QUEEN
OF
The Reapers

Copyright © 2022 by Jessa Halliwell

All rights reserved.

No part of this book may be reproduced in any form or by any electronic or mechanical means, including information storage and retrieval systems, without written permission from the author, except for the use of brief quotations in a book review.

❃ Created with Vellum

CONTENTS

Playlist	v
Trigger Warning	vii
Prologue	1
Chapter 1	7
Chapter 2	21
Chapter 3	31
Chapter 4	37
Chapter 5	47
Chapter 6	55
Chapter 7	63
Chapter 8	75
Chapter 9	81
Chapter 10	87
Chapter 11	103
Chapter 12	111
Chapter 13	123
Chapter 14	139
Chapter 15	155
Chapter 16	165
Chapter 17	185
Chapter 18	195
Chapter 19	205
Chapter 20	219
Chapter 21	229
Chapter 22	237
Wrath of The Reapers Excerpt	245
Stay in Touch	257
Books by Jessa	259
A Note From Jessa	261
About Jessa	263

PLAYLIST

The Only High by The Veronicas
Angels Don't Cry by Ellise
Numb by Carlie Hanson
PSYCHO by Aviva
Savage by Bahari (Nightcore Remix)
Play with Fire by Sam Tinnesz, Yacht Money
Empire by Neoni
Cravin' by Stileto, Kendyle Paige
DARKSIDE by Neoni
Villain of My Own Story by Unlike Pluto
Stockholm Syndrome by Aracana
Dangerous by The Tech Thieves, Besomorph
Flames by R3HAB, ZAYN, Jungleboi
Serial Killer by Moncrieff, JUDGE
Joke's On You by Charlotte Lawrence

TRIGGER WARNING

The Reapers are not good men. They have no moral code and they certainly have no limits. If you're looking for a story where the heroine turns the bad boys good, well then this story isn't for you. This is the world of The Reapers and the only way to survive is to play by their rules.

The Reapers of Caspian Hills is a Dark Romance and features content that some readers may find disturbing. Visit the author's website for a detailed list of potential triggers.

PROLOGUE

FEAR IS SUCH A FICKLE EMOTION AND WE, AS HUMANS, FEAR so many things.

Change. Death. Love.

We get so blinded by our fears that if we aren't careful; they end up consuming us. Swallowing us whole. Leaving nothing more than a shell of a person who's too scared to trust anyone, especially themselves.

Fear is what led me into the world of The Reapers.

To save his life, my shit-for-brains stepfather, Malcolm, sacrificed my little sister to the devil, or rather, devils; The Reapers of Caspian Hills. The arrangement he made was simple: The Reapers get to keep Alex, and in exchange, he gets to keep his life. But, as with any sordid deal, nothing is ever quite that easy.

There was one determining factor The Reapers didn't consider. One factor that could have changed their entire outlook on Malcolm's tempting offer.

My sister wasn't just some nameless girl that no one would miss. She was loved, she had a family, and there was someone willing to fight for her. Someone who would stop at nothing to protect her. And that someone was me.

Growing up, I was always Alex's protector. I shielded her from our mother's cruel reign and when that stopped; I shielded her from the fallout of her father's addiction. I wasn't about to stand idly by and let some low-life criminal assholes take her away. She was the only family I had left, and I wasn't willing to let her go without a fight.

Offering myself in my sister's place was borderline suicidal, but I willingly walked into the lion's den, anyway. The Reapers couldn't break me anymore than I'd already been broken and while I was terrified of what they'd do to me, nothing scared me more than the thought of what they'd do to her.

The last thing I wanted was for my sweet little sister to end up as cold and jaded as I was. She deserved a better life, and I was ready to do whatever it took to give it to her.

I knew the risks when I stepped through the doors of their mansion. Knew they could and would try to break me behind those walls. What I failed to take into consideration was just how much I might like it.

Atlas, Ezra, Cyrus, and Tristan Cole evoked feelings within me I forgot existed. Feelings I had securely locked away as a child. And while every interaction with them was confusing, jarring, and sometimes painful, each of them made me come alive.

I planned to fight The Reapers tooth and nail. To do whatever it took to keep my sister safe. The one thing I never planned on was catching feelings for them.

By an ironic twist of fate, the dangerous men I thought would ruin me ended up being the only men I could rely on. The only men, besides my late father, I could see myself trusting.

But the shitty thing about fear is, just when you think you've conquered it, that bitch rears its ugly head again and, well, old habits die hard.

The minute I thought Alex was in danger, all of my newfound allegiance to The Reapers went out the fucking window. I thought I trusted them, but when it came down to it, I couldn't bring myself to ask for their help.

Sure, they played nice around me, but bringing my sister around them was an entirely different ballgame. Everything I'd done up to that point was to protect her, and I still didn't trust that they'd keep her safe.

Like an idiot, I snuck away from The Reapers and fell headfirst into a trap.

Without my bad-boy cavalry at my side, I was seriously outnumbered and completely fucked. No pun intended. If it weren't for The Reapers busting through the door and literally saving my ass, I'd be lying dead in a ditch somewhere with no one to blame but my stupid choices.

I didn't deserve the second chance they gave me, or the third, if I'm honest. But this time around, I refuse to let my fear fuck things up again. The Reapers are my happily ever after and I won't let anyone stand in the way of that, not even me.

ONE

Stevie

THE TIRES SCREECH IN PROTEST AS EZRA SLAMS HIS FOOT ON the brake and pulls us to the side of the road. A brown cloud of dirt and debris settles around us as we come to a stop next to a long line of giant redwoods. I look at Atlas, Tristan, and Cyrus, but they don't seem phased by the unplanned pit-stop. Then again, they too probably need a moment to digest my request.

"No." Tristan says with a dismissive shake of his head. "It's a s… stupid idea."

Instead of letting myself react to his harsh refusal, I focus on the hem of the onyx suit jacket, barely grazing my thighs. The luxurious wool fabric is soft to the touch and as the other voices in the car chime in to the debate, I mindlessly run my thumbs along its pristine seams. It's a pointless distraction, but I'm desperate to focus on anything other than the chaos erupting around me, even if I am the catalyst.

It's been over an hour since we left Maria's Cantina, but there's still a hint of violence in the air. Almost as if it's haunting us. Refusing to let us forget the massacre we left behind.

"In all fairness," Cyrus drawls, casting a pointed look at his twin, "when have *you* ever thought any risk was worth taking?"

The icy glare Tristan shoots at Cyrus is enough to knock the wind out of me, but Cyrus just cocks a brow and chuckles. "What's the matter?" He asks. "Hit a little too close to home?"

The tension crackling between the two of them is thick enough to cut with a knife, and of course, I'm the one seated in the middle of their battlefield.

Aesthetically, the twins are nearly identical. The same piercing emerald eyes, the same dark disheveled hair you can't help but want to run your fingers through, and the same disarming good looks that should be illegal in such dangerous men. The similarities between the two stop there.

Cyrus is like fire. Explosive. Dynamic. And consuming. He could easily light you up and make you come alive, but on that same note, if you do him dirty, he'll engulf you in his inferno and burn your ass beyond recognition.

Tristan is like ice. Cold. Impenetrable. And unpredictable.

Getting through to him is like trying to chisel your way through thick walls of ice. Once you get there, the payoff will be worth it. But that's if and only if you can survive his frigid bite.

"Tris has a point." Atlas says, raking his fingers through his hair as he leans back into the passenger seat. "We have enough on our plate."

It doesn't take a genius to figure out I'm the 'enough' he's referring to. And as they each subconsciously glance my way, my suspicions are all but confirmed.

The weight of their stares burn into my skin, and the icy blast from the air conditioner does nothing to soothe the heat. Sweat coats the small of my back as little beads of moisture trickle down my spine. I'm in over my head, but letting them see my discomfort isn't an option. This conversation is too damn important.

Gnawing on my nails, I glance at the clock on the dashboard and grimace. It's only been a few minutes since Ezra pulled over, but the ensuing argument feels like it's been going on for hours. I know they care about me. Probably now, more than ever. But the problem is, this isn't about me, it's about her. And she isn't something they ever planned on.

"She's a liability." Ezra says, cutting into the conversation. He flicks the ash of his cigarette out the window and pulls another long drag before continuing. "Jessie used her as bait. It's only a matter of time before someone else does the same."

She's not a liability, she's family.

I feel my composure slipping and I know it's only a matter of time before my anger finds its way out. They're treating my sister like she's an inconvenience. Like she's some fucking business decision they need to weigh out. Like she isn't even a fucking person at all.

"We could s... send her away." Tristan says, looking down at me. "Keep her safe from this s... shit."

I almost scoff at his offer, but I stop myself short and maintain my cool composure. If the roles were reversed, I doubt he'd be so eager to send any of his brothers away. I'm sure they'd all fight with everything they had to stay together. I'm doing exactly what any of them would.

Tristan hooks his finger under my chin and tilts my head up. "S... Stevie, look at me." He says, locking his dark emerald eyes with mine. "We can keep her s... safe. Don't you want that?"

Goddamnit. He's putting me in an impossible situation. Deep down, I know he's right. My priority has always been to keep her safe. The only way to guarantee her safety is to keep her as far away from The Reapers as possible. They would never hurt her, but their enemies might. Sending her away *is* the smart choice, but he of all people should know, the smartest choice isn't always the right one.

"No." I sigh, avoiding his eyes as I jerk my chin out of his grip. "I know my sister. If I try to push her away, she'll just fight her way back to me. It won't work."

I don't need to look into his eyes to feel his disappointment.

"Fine." He spits, looking out into the dense forest surrounding the G-Wagon. "Don't come crying to us when she ends up f... fucking dead." He says the last sentence under his breath, but with the deafening silence filling the SUV, he may as well have screamed it.

"Look." Atlas says, pulling everyone's attention on him.

"It's been a long day and emotions are high. Priority right now is going home and getting cleaned up. We can discuss all of this shit later."

Fuck. Fuck. Fuck.

When Atlas gives an order, they all follow his command like gospel. We're going home and no amount of pleading will get them to change their minds.

I want to trust that we'll continue this conversation when we get home, but after watching this discussion go up in flames, it's clear none of them want to bring Alex in. To them, she's a risk not worth taking.

"I'm not going home." I say, doing my best to keep my voice from wavering. "I'll walk if I have to, but I'm going back for her."

This could be my last shot at retrieving Alex. I have to fight them on this, even if they end up hating me for it.

I shift my gaze to the left and look at Tristan expectantly. The icy glare he shoots back at me stings, but I keep my face even.. There's a challenge in his emerald eyes, and I know there's no way I'm getting past him without a fight, so I shift my focus to the lesser of the two evils, his twin, Cyrus.

"Cy, can you let me out?" I ask, keeping my voice soft to disguise the frustration brewing within me.

Cyrus doesn't bother to look at me as he shoots out his clipped response. "Not happening, Princess."

What the hell.

"Cyrus." I say, gritting my teeth to keep my anger under control. "I don't have time for your little mind games. I need you to let me out. Now."

"No." His response is short, but the venom behind the word stings.

"Cyrus." I whisper, moistening my lips. "You can't be serious right now."

He clenches his jaw and lets out an exaggerated sigh.

"What makes you think I'm joking?" He snaps, narrowing his eyes at me. "What? Are we supposed to be your little fucking lapdogs now because we saved you?"

"That's not—"

"No, it is." He says, cutting me off as he inches towards my face. "We aren't those men, Princess."

"I just thought—"

"You thought what? That things changed? That the men who own you suddenly transformed from monsters into princes? I hate to be the bearer of bad news, P, but we're still The Reapers. The dangerous men you offered yourself up to on a silver fucking platter. You are ours. To own. To fuck. And to do whatever the hell else we want with. That hasn't changed, P, and it never will."

The cool veneer I was trying to cling on to immediately shatters. Fuck this and fuck all of them. If that's how they see me, then why am I even trying to get them to understand? If all I am to them is a piece of property, they'll never care about how I feel. Why would they? They have the power to do as they please and use my body any way they see fit.

No. The only way I'm getting back to my sister is if I fight for her. And if it's a fight they want, it's a fight they'll fucking get.

Like a flash of lightning, I lunge out of my seat and shove my way towards the door. In the back of my mind, I know it's pointless. Cyrus and Tristan can easily overpower me, but I refuse to back down. I have to fight for Alex, even if it is futile.

Constricting arms tangle around my body, but I don't stop fighting. For their parts, Cyrus and Tristan try to stop me without injuring me, but my kicks and shoves are getting more violent by the second. I hate them for what they're doing to me, and I hate myself for how far this is going.

"Stop!" The twins bark in unison, but I'm too far gone to listen to their orders. I've been constrained and restricted my entire fucking life and their blatant disregard for my needs just a lit a twenty-year-old fuse.

I scratch and I claw and I push and I shove until I can barely tell where my feet and hands are landing. Other voices start mixing with their protests and more hands are on me, but I block them out. I'm getting out of this fucking car now.

"GODDAMNIT STEVIE, THAT'S ENOUGH!" Atlas booms, pounding his heavy hand against the dash.

The anger and violence in his voice snaps me back to reality. I jerk my head in his direction and freeze. Fiery rage fills his eyes, and I can't help but cower under his narrowed gaze.

"Stop acting like a petulant fucking child." He spits, his breathing labored from trying to pry me off of his brothers. "We're going home. Now. End of discussion."

My bottom lip quivers and before I can block it out, an all too familiar emotion grabs a hold of me and pulls me under. Fear. Only this time the person terrifying me isn't my mother, it's Atlas.

I feel his anger and disappointment all around me, coating my skin and engulfing me. I'm drowning in it. I'm ashamed and, as much as I hate looking weak, I can't stop the tears from welling in my eyes.

"That's not my fucking home." I sputter, choking on my

words as my vision blurs with unshed tears. "That mansion is just a gilded fucking cage and you know it."

I'm screaming now and my emotions are swirling through me like a tornado of rage, shame, guilt, and sorrow. I can't hold it in any longer and the words are spewing out of me uncontrollably.

"You guys think you're so strong. The fucking Reapers. The men who elicit fear in everyone they meet. But you know what I think? I think you're four scared little boys trapped in the bodies of full-grown men. You control and manipulate and torture and trick your way into power because that's the closest thing to love and acceptance you'll ever feel. You think I'm some weak little girl that needs a prince to save her, but newsflash, I don't need your kindness, I don't need your love, and I especially don't need you. The only fucking thing I need right now is—"

My words die off the second I take in each of their pained expressions. Regret sinks into my stomach and festers, making me relive all the bitter words I threw at them. I want to apologize. To tell them I didn't mean any of it, but I can't even stomach the idea of facing them. I can barely breathe, let alone speak.

My eyes flicker to each of them and I study their hard features. Cyrus' brows are pulled together in a scowl and his fists are tightly clenched as he stares daggers at me. Tristan's eyes are low and he presses his lips in a hard line as he avoids looking at me altogether. Atlas' head is cocked and his mouth is slightly ajar, almost as if he can't believe I'm the one who spewed such venomous words. And Ezra is looking at me with a question in his eyes. Like he no longer knows what to think about me.

Hurting them feels like I'm ripping a piece of my own heart out, but my concern for my sister outweighs any feelings I have for them. It has to. I'm all she has left.

I glance at Ezra and catch his reflection in the mirror. He's looking out his window now, but as he pulls his cigarette up to his lips and takes a slow drag, his stormy grey eyes land on mine. *God, he is going to kill me. What the hell was I thinking?*

"Finish." Ezra orders, studying my expression from his rear-view mirror. "Might as well get it all out now."

He's right. My feeble attempt to put out the fire my words ignited was pointless. I've already said the worst of it and it's only fair that they hear my full thoughts before they decide what happens next. "The only thing I need right now is my sister." I breathe, pulling in a shaky breath. "She's the only family I have left. I'm ready to move forward, but she's the one part of my past I can't leave behind."

The second I release the words, it feels like a heavy weight has been lifted from my chest. Atlas, Ezra, Cyrus, & Tristan sit silent for a moment and stare off into the forest, taking a few minutes to mull over everything I said. I keep my eyes low and wait for a response. I think about elaborating further, but I already said more than enough as it is.

After several minutes of uncomfortable silence, Atlas is the first to speak up.

"Call her." He says, spitting the words out as if they taste rancid in his mouth. "Have her head to Alessandro's. Our men will take it from there."

"I can't." I say, my voice sounding smaller than it ever has. "I have no way of reaching her."

"Here." Tristan barks, carelessly tossing the familiar rose gold iPhone on my thigh. "Have at it."

Seeing my confiscated phone only fortifies the wall my outburst built between us. I avoid thinking about our past, but seeing my cell phone serves as a healthy reminder of how this started. Of how we started.

A few weeks ago, I was just their stubborn toy, and they were the men determined to put me in my place. Feelings have changed between us, sure, but the power balance needs to change if this is ever going to work. I'm not their toy anymore and it's about damn time they started treating me like it.

"You've had this on you this whole time..."

It's more of a statement than a question, but Tristan's casual shrug gives me all the answers I need. I'm not sure why it bothers me. It's typical controlling Reaper behavior. They want to keep me alive. That much is obvious. But The Reapers won't suddenly change who they are just because they want me around. Sadistic tigers don't change their stripes.

"Thanks, but I meant what I said." I say, slipping my phone into the jacket's pocket. "I can't call her. Jessie destroyed her phone. The only way I can reach her is if I go to her."

"Let me guess." Ezra scoffs, flashing me a deadly smile as he crushes his cigarette against the side mirror and flicks the butt to the ground. "You want this little reunion of yours to happen now."

Every fiber of my being is on edge as I try to predict what he'll do next. I know Ez, in a lot of ways, better than his brothers do, but that doesn't mean he's predictable. Ezra may care about me in his own twisted way, but the monster within him will always dictate what he does. It's as much a part of him as the tattoos coating his body.

Before Ezra can speak again, Atlas cuts in. "Okay." He says, rubbing his temple as he pulls a cigar from the glove box. "We'll bring Alex in." He offers, lighting it up and puffing out a thick cloud of smoke. "But if something happens to her from here on out, it's on you. Not us."

"That's fair." I reply, looking into each of their hard faces. "I'm the one that's bringing her in. So whatever happens to Al is on me."

Before I can even finish my thoughts, Ezra whips the G-Wagon around in a sharp u-turn and smashes his foot against the accelerator. The tires screech in response, kicking up a storm of dust as he jerks the car back onto the narrow road. His white knuckles angrily grip the steering wheel and it takes everything in me not to panic as he guns it down the hill.

We're going too fast and his brothers aren't even reacting to his antics, seemingly in their own worlds. I latch onto my seatbelt for dear life as he swerves dangerously down the winding cliff-side road. He's always threatened to hurt me, but I never imagined he'd try to kill us all like this.

I catch Ezra's stormy eyes in the rear-view mirror and hold his gaze, silently willing him to slow the hell down. I search for the Ezra I know, the one I sacrificed my mind, body, and soul to over the last few weeks, but I don't find him. The monster is the only one staring back and, as luck would have it, the fucker is pissed.

"Something wrong, Angel?" Ezra asks, his silky voice like a siren song for my stupid heart. The voice that chases my demons away and has the innate ability to soothe my nerves.

It's hard to believe it belongs to the same monster sitting behind the wheel.

Ezra thrives on the fear of others and no matter how much he scares me, fear is the one thing I can never afford to show him. Not if I want him to treat me as his equal and not if I want to be his.

Bringing my eyes back to his nearly black ones, I face him with my head held high and give him my full attention. He stares back at me unflinchingly as the car continues to swerve in and out of the opposing lane. Oncoming cars swerve around us with their horns blaring, but I don't even flinch. It's reckless, but I refuse to break his gaze, even at the expense of our safety. We're in a war of wills and I need to show him that not only am I unafraid of the beast, but that I fully embrace its chaos.

Bring it on, monster.

After a few minutes of heart-stopping close calls, Ezra is the first to break our stare-off, and as he does, a slow smirk spreads across his face.

"Clever girl." He remarks, locking his eyes back on the road. "Angel, don't mistake this kindness as a sign of weakness. Leaving us was never one of your options."

He doesn't need to elaborate any further for me to understand the threat behind his words. There will be no leaving The Reapers. Not now and not ever.

TWO

Stevie

We arrive at our destination less than an hour later. The sun is low in the sky, creating a beautiful backdrop to the hideous scene appearing before us.

The night we checked in, Dina's Quality Inn looked desolate, but in the broad daylight, the place looks downright depressing. The dull-brown two-story building is coated in a thick layer of dirt, adding discolored blotches to the already faded and weathered exterior. Time hasn't been friendly to

Dina's. Every window on the building is missing its screen, its curtains, or a combination of the two.

"I can't believe I left her here." It's the only thing I can stomach to say. The guys say nothing in response, but they don't need to. It's written all over their faces.

It's just after 4pm and the place is a virtual ghost town, with only a handful of run-down cars stationed in the parking lot. The few guests we see hanging around the property seem to be completely in their own world. Too high out of their minds to give the five of us anything more than a brief glance as we slowly creep past them.

"Keep going." I say, directing Ezra towards the backside of the building. "It's just a little further."

My stomach dips with each room we pass. Room 121… Room 122… Room 123…

It's only been six weeks since the last time I spoke to my sister, but because of everything that's happened, it feels like years. I'm not the same girl that left her here and after everything I've been through, I don't know if I ever will be again.

"There." I say, pointing to the room number I etched in my brain. "That's the room, 132."

Ezra pulls the SUV into an empty parking spot directly in front of the room and kills the engine. I make a move to exit, but a muscular arm holds me in place. *Tristan.*

"Clear to the left." Ezra says, keeping his eyes on the few people roaming nearby.

"Clear on the rear." Cyrus says, casting a glance at Atlas.

"Good over here." Atlas says, pulling his pistol out of its holster. "Tris, go with her." He orders, keeping his eyes on the door. "In and out."

Tristan unbuckles his seatbelt and climbs out of the car.

After taking a deep breath, I do the same and slide out of the car and into the oppressive heat to join him. Tristan holds the door open for me, and as soon as my bare feet land on the hot pavement, his powerful arms lift me into the air.

I'm surprised by his sudden closeness and I'm not sure how to feel about it. But before I get too wrapped up in my thoughts, Tristan speaks up. "There are needles on the ground." He explains, wrapping my legs tightly around his waist.

"Oh." I breathe, chastising myself for assuming there was more to it than that.

Tristan steps forward, and I fight the instinct to wrap my arms around his neck. This is business for him, nothing more, and it isn't fair for me to pretend like everything is okay between us after everything I said.

Spotting the hesitance on my face, he stops mid stride and levels his eyes on me. "Cut the shit." He says, pulling my arms around his neck. "I know what you're thinking. But none of this changes anything between us."

"It doesn't?"

"No. You belong with us." He says, shifting me closer. "Your s... sister doesn't, but I can't blame you for wanting her t... to."

Maybe Tristan's right. Maybe the blowout in the car is my glaring sign my two worlds can't mix. My world with The Reapers and my world with Alex are two very different things. I have no business expecting them to collide without a little fallout. But if there's even a tiny chance of it working, I have to try.

Once we reach the door, Tristan sets me down and takes two wide steps back. As much as I want him close, I'm relieved he gives me a little space. All 75 inches of him would intimidate anyone that up close and the last thing I want to do is scare the shit out of Alex before she gets a real chance to get to know them.

I rap my knuckles against the thin burgundy door and wait for her to answer as my heart thunders in my chest.

Nothing.

Come on, Al. Answer the door.

I knock again, harder this time, and wait.

Still nothing.

Not willing to give up, I step up to the dust coated window and start pounding on the glass. *Maybe she can't hear me.*

"Al, it's me." I call out, banging my fists harder against the glass. "Open up."

Still no response.

Thanks to the motel's shoddy craftsmanship, the heavy drapery adorning the windows doesn't quite close all the way, creating a little pocket large enough for me to peek inside. Peering through the glass, I search the small space and find the room just as I remembered it. Four unsightly beige walls and a simple oak bed and dresser set that's too large for the already cramped space. The hideous rust-colored comforter looks freshly made, but the familiar clothes strewn around the room and the boxes of takeout perched on the edge of the bed give me hope. Alex isn't here, but she definitely was.

"S... see anything?" Tristan asks, moving closer to me.

"No." I say, shaking my head as I back away from the window. "She's not here. But it doesn't make sense. She's not in school anymore. She has no one else. Where the hell else could she have gone?"

My own words punch me straight in the gut. *She has no one else.*

Guilt seeps into me and grips me in a vise. *Fuck. Fuck. Fuck.* In the last two months, not only did I abandon my little sister at some shit-hole motel, but I missed her eighteenth birthday and her graduation. We were stuck between an armed drug-addict and a group of dangerous assholes, but I'm the one who decided. I'm the one who left.

Pushing the self-deprecating thoughts aside, I shift my focus to the front office. I'm not leaving this shitty motel without my sister and if anyone knows her whereabouts, it's the nosy lady working the front desk. She gave us the fifth degree when we checked in, and has been watching us like a fucking hawk through her little window ever since we pulled in to the parking lot.

I march towards the front office, but I don't make it far. Before I'm even an arms-length away, I feel Tristan's hand wrap around my elbow. "Where d… do you think you're going?" He asks, whipping my body around to face him.

"To find my sister." I spit back, shaking off his grip.

I flick my eyes up to cut him a vicious glare and almost immediately pause at the sight in front of me. Cyrus, Atlas, and Ezra have joined him, and are looking at me with the same clenched jaws and narrowed eyes as their brother. The family resemblance has never been more striking.

"No." Atlas orders, stepping forward to block my way. "You're covered in blood, and my jacket is the only piece of clothing on your body. Coming to her room was our one allowance, but we aren't wasting any more time on this shit. You're done for tonight."

The finality of his words piss me off. I wouldn't be in this state if it weren't for Jessie's obsession with him and his brothers. In fact, if they never made that stupid deal with Malcolm, Alex and I would still be together now. I would've never met them, but at least Al and I would be safe. This is all their fault.

"What is this sick fascination with ordering me around?" I ask, glaring up at Atlas with my arms wrapped across my chest. "You can't just tell me to jump and expect me to ask how high. That's not how a relationship works."

There, I said it. The thought that's been weighing on my mind ever since we gave this thing between us a real go. Our relationship has changed, but the way he and his brothers treat me hasn't. They can't keep treating me like their property and expect me just to roll over and take it.

"That's how we work." Tristan interjects, stepping next to Atlas. "Especially when it's f… for your own good."

"But Alex—" I protest.

"Alex can wait." Cyrus asserts, flanking his twin's side.

They're forming a stupid fucking blockade, and all I want to do is thrash against it. I look towards Ezra, the only one not caging me like an animal. He's just as angry, but he has to back me on this. Someone has to.

"Ez?" I ask, putting him on the spot.

Ezra smiles before answering me, and my hope blossoms. *I knew he'd pull through for me.*

"We either take you willingly," he says, dropping his smile as cruelty seeps into his voice, "or unwillingly. Either way, you're coming with us." The hope I held on to splinters into a million pieces.

Why am I even trying to reason with them? These aren't rational men who are going to sit here and hear me out.

They're going to do what they want and when they want, and fighting them will only make things worse. The best thing I can do right now is stay in their good graces and hope they give me another chance to come back for Al. But when have I ever done what's best for me?

Instead of arguing, I do the only thing I can do. The only thing that sits right in my gut. *I run.*

I cut around Ezra and gun it for the front office. It's stupid. It's the dumbest decision I can make, but I'm in fight-or-flight mode and, well, I'm choosing flight.

As soon as they realize I'm running, the four of them immediately split into two groups with military precision. Tris and Cy cut around the back of the building while Atlas and Ezra chase me as I weave through the parking lot.

"Stevie, stop!" Atlas yells, his powerful voice sounding farther away than I expect.

A smug smile forms on my lips. *Looks like I'm going to make it to the front desk after all.*

"No." I call out, glancing behind me to find him and Ezra scowling a good twenty feet away.

They look pissed, but they'll get over it. I'll make up for everything after I get my answers.

"Goddamnit," Atlas curses, "stop!"

He sounds angry, more angry than he's ever sounded before and that's saying something. But I can't bring myself to stop now, even if I wanted to. Besides, as it stands now, I'm already in deep shit for running. If I make it to the office, at least I'll be able to leave with a lead and a bit of dignity.

"Angel!" Ezra yells with such urgency it terrifies me. Ezra may be the craziest of them all, but he never yells. He's always teetering on the thin line between cool and detached, but not once has he ever yelled at me. I whip my head in their direction so fast that for a second, my head spins.

"Watch out!" Atlas barks, gesturing at whatever is in front of me.

My brain understands his message a split-second too late. Just as I turn to look ahead of me, my bare foot clips a cement wheel stop and the force of the impact sends my body crashing into the rough asphalt.

My bare knees and palms break most of my fall before my body rolls to an excruciating stop behind a rusty white van. The pain shooting up and down my body is mind-numbing, but from what I can tell, nothing is broken.

Tears sting in my eyes as a mixture of pain and embarrassment hits me hard. *Why the fuck did I run?*

Atlas' strong arms lift me into his chest and I try to fight him off. The last thing I want is his fucking pity. Not now and especially not this way.

"Get the fuck off of me!" I cry, flailing my fists at his chest.

Ignoring my weak demands, Atlas walks us back to the SUV in silence. He gently places me into the backseat and buckles me in with his face void of emotion. Ever so calmly, he grabs a tiny bottle from the glove-box and shakes two pills into the palm of his hand and hands them to me.

"Take them." He says through clenched teeth.

There's no point in resisting anymore, and I pop them back without protest. As the dry pills slide down my throat, the fight within me flickers out. I'm not getting Alex back tonight, and after what I just pulled, I may never get to see her again.

Good job, Dumbass.

THREE

Cyrus

"She still sleeping?"

I peel my eyes away from the passing city streets and glance at Atlas. It takes a second for me to register his question and as I do; I release a heavy sigh.

"Yeah." I offer, glancing at the woman nestled against my side. "The painkillers are doing their job."

Atlas gives me a quick nod before returning his attention to his phone. Guaranteed, he's missed hundreds of emails just in the few hours we've been unreachable and is doing his best to catch-up.

While we run our syndicate like a democracy, with each of us having equal say in every pertinent decision, Atlas is our leader and when it comes down to it, he's who we all look to for answers. The one tasked with making the tough calls. Others may envy the power he holds, but the three of us know how heavy the responsibility of running a highly organized crime syndicate is.

It isn't all guns and intimidation bullshit. In fact, most of the time, the job is highly political and pretty fucking boring. Days filled with business meetings, contracts, and email after email. Aside from the legalities, heading The Reapers is like running a Fortune 500 company and At is right up there with some of the most powerful men in the world.

But in the criminal world, it takes more than business savvy and a degree to succeed. After working his way up in the ranks since he was sixteen, there is no one who deserves the power more than Atlas. He alone is the reason The Organization allowed four Half-Mexican, Half-Swedish kids with no Russian familial ties to run their second largest stronghold on the west coast six years running. Our revenues come only second to The Devil's Disciples who run a pretty impressive operation in Los Angeles. Despite the odds stacked against us, Atlas has kept us together and kept us whole.

"Should we discuss the s… sister shit now?" Tristan asks, bringing up the topic we'd all been avoiding.

"There's nothing to discuss." Atlas mutters, scrolling through his phone. "If we deny her sister, Stevie will fight."

"Bringing her s… sister into our world is dangerous."

Tristan says, keeping his voice low. "We need to cut this s... shit off before it goes any f... further."

I shake my head dismissively. "We do that, we lose her." Maybe not physically. Ezra meant every word he said earlier, but the Stevie we know would disappear. If she was ever really here to begin with.

Despite how it worked out, allowing Stevie into our world was a stupid decision. We assumed we could easily discard her without a second thought, that she was just a toy we wouldn't give a fuck about in a few weeks. But the fiery little thing got under our skin and now there's no way in hell any of us will let her go.

In a lot of ways, Stevie terrifies me. She's a wild card in every sense of the word. She alone holds the power to become our greatest ally, but on that same note, she could easily become the greatest enemy we've ever faced. The worst part is, I don't think any of us could tell the difference until it was too late.

Every single one of us would let her destroy us from the inside out if she felt inspired to do so. We would sit back and watch her rip our entire empire to shreds and still give her a smile like pathetic bastards we are. She has us in the palm of her hands, and having that much power over men like us is a very scary thing.

"Then what the fuck are we s... supposed to do..." Tristan murmurs, cracking his knuckles.

"We give Alex the choice." Atlas says, bringing all of our attention to him. "We bring her in, lay everything out on the table, and she gets to decide what she wants to do."

"And if Alex doesn't want this life?" I ask, cocking my head in At's direction.

"Then we send her away and Stevie will have to accept it."

Ezra scoffs, shaking his head at the three of us like we're the most gullible assholes he's ever seen. "That's assuming she doesn't just follow her. None of you have taken into consideration what would really happen if her sister doesn't want this. If forced to choose, Stevie will take her little sister over us without question. We could try to stop her, but as long as her sister is out there, she'll keep fighting us to get to her."

"You don't know that." Atlas retorts, setting his phone down to glare at him.

"Don't I? Alex is the reason Stevie came into our world to begin with. If she was willing to risk her life for her sister then, who's to say she wouldn't risk us to do the same?"

As tough as it is to hear, Ezra has a point and we all know it.

The car fills with a heavy silence as we cut the discussion short and the three of us mull over his words. While I think, I lean against my door and look out at the evergreens off in the distance, slowly drawing closer.

Caspian Hills is unlike any other city in the world. Within a twenty-mile radius you can find a bustling downtown, a scenic hillside forest with breath-taking ocean views, and a pristine beach complete with a seaside boardwalk. It's where we've lived and worked for the last seven years, but it never truly felt like home until Stevie came into our world.

She's impulsive, and a bit unhinged, but I could say the same for any of us. Having her in our lives gives us something to look forward to each day, and as I look down at her sleeping form, I know in my gut I'm not willing to give her up.

"We eliminate the option." I say, feeling the sincerity of the words in my chest. I'd do anything to keep Stevie, and if Alex becomes a threat, she needs to be eliminated. It's as simple as that.

"Eliminate." Tristan sneers, looking at me in disbelief. "We can't kill her s… sister to suit our needs."

"Baby brother, have you forgotten?" Ezra smirks, drumming his thumbs against the steering wheel. "It's part of the family business. Besides, it's not just us we're thinking about. As long as Alex is out there, she's a danger to our girl and when it comes down to it, I'll do whatever it takes to keep Stevie safe."

"Even killing her own blood." Tris spits, crossing his arms over his chest. "Unbelievable."

"It won't come to that." Atlas chastises, glaring at the three of us. "Alex will choose to stay, we'll make sure of it."

"And if she d… doesn't?" Tristan asks, his brows creasing into a scowl.

"If she doesn't." Ezra hisses, glaring at Tristan from his rearview mirror. "I'll keep you blissfully unaware, baby brother, so you can still sleep well at night knowing you had nothing to do with it."

FOUR

"Put me down, you asshole."

From the second I pulled her out of the car, Stevie hasn't stopped complaining. Part of me wants to drop her on her ass and watch her limp up the driveway with her tail between her legs. The other part of me, the stupid overprotective fuckhead part, would rather deal with her relentless stubbornness than watch her feel another second of pain. The second part wins.

"Not going t... to happen, Pet." I retort, shifting her body higher in my arms. She glares up at me with narrowed eyes.

"What happened to 'baby'?" She scoffs, bitterness coating her tongue. Stevie is being her usual stubborn ass self, but after the shit that went down tonight, I've had about as much of her bullshit as I can handle.

"You're the one f… fighting us like a rabid fucking animal." I say, glaring down at her. "You want to act like a f… fucking pet, then we'll treat you like one."

Silence falls between the two of us as she soaks in my words.

"I can walk, you know." She says, glaring up at me. "By all means, don't let me hold you back from your little family meeting." She nods her head towards the window of the study for emphasis. "I'm sure they're making more decisions for my life in there. Wouldn't want you to miss that."

"God. Why are you s… so fucking stubborn." I grunt, refusing to look down at her again as I continue our climb up the driveway. "Learn how to accept help when it's given t… to you."

She jerks her head towards me and stabs her index finger into my chest.

"Maybe you should learn how to listen when a girl tells you no. I need to find Alex and wasting time with you isn't going to make that happen any faster."

I stop moving and glare at her, *hard*.

"Wasting t… time, huh?" I ask, looming over her. "You think this is a waste of f… fucking time?"

She says nothing in response, so I continue. The words shoot out of me and cut into her like knives.

"You're s… so hell bent on taking care of everyone else. On making s.. sure every other person in your world is okay.

But t... tell me, who the fuck takes care of you, Stevie? Huh?"

I see a war forming behind her eyes. She wants to fight back. To tell me I'm fucking wrong. But she knows I'm right. She doesn't say so, but it's written all over her face. Her mouth falls open and her wide eyes shine with unshed tears.

I know Stevie, so I focus my attention back on the house to give her a second to recollect herself. She may be reluctantly accepting my help, but she'd never forgive me if I don't let her have her pride. It's one of the few things in this world she holds sacred.

"Ezra is going back t... to the motel." I offer, picking up my pace again as if nothing happened. "As s... soon as she shows up, he'll bring her home."

The rest of the walk into the house is silent as an unspoken peace treaty settles over us. I said everything I wanted to say and Stevie seems too stuck in her own head to want to say anything else. We made finding her sister a priority, which, based on the look in her dazed eyes, came as a shock. But it shouldn't have. We may be morally corrupt assholes who linger on the outskirts of law, but we are men of our word. We told her we'd retrieve her sister and we're doing everything we can to keep that promise.

Once we get inside, I make my way up the long staircase and chance a glance down at her. I expect to see the anger on her face return, but when I see her, I find nothing of the sort. Stevie looks lost, like a girl who's just gone through hell and barely made it out alive. The skin around her wrists is raw and I can already see the bruising finger prints on her arms forming. I wish we could resurrect the bastards that hurt her, only to slaughter them all over again for what they did.

I haven't pressed her for details, but it's hard not to think about what would've happened had we shown up a few seconds later. She's strong. So much stronger than my brothers and I in a lot of ways, but she's still so goddamn fragile. So fucking human.

I could've lost her before I ever really had her. Before we could figure out whatever the hell this was between us. She loves Atlas and apparently has, for quite some time, she embraces Ezra with all his idiosyncrasies, and has an unspoken bond with Cyrus. But with me, all we have is miscommunication after miscommunication. Fight after fucking fight. I want what's best for her. I just haven't been the best at showing it.

We close in on her room and I know this is where our peace treaty will end. I'll go back to my room without ever telling her how I really feel and she'll go back to hers, despising the men that forced her away from her sister. Given their connections, my brothers may get back in her good graces, but I'll always be the asshole that didn't want her sister. That fate was sealed the second she denied my offer.

We're almost at her door and I can't help but slow my pace. She feels so fucking good in my arms, but in a few seconds, they'll be empty again. Fuck. I'm not ready to let her go. To let this peace treaty between us end. I want more of her. I need it. So, like the selfish fuck I am, I keep walking.

"Where are you taking me?" Stevie asks, noticing we've moved past her bedroom.

"My bathroom." I say, thinking on my feet. "We have t… to clean your wounds before they get infected."

It isn't a bad idea. Who knows what kind of shit was on the ground in that parking lot.

As soon as we step into the bathroom, her lips twitch with a hint of a smile. She likes what she sees, and I don't blame her. The interior designers got a little carried away with the elements of this space and this bathroom is the most extravagant room in the house by far. They tiled the large space floor to ceiling with natural slate gray stone and set up natural waterfalls throughout the space, giving the room an atmospheric, almost grotto-like energy. To complete the design, they set an in-ground jetted tub into the stone floor, making it look more like a natural hot spring than a hot tub.

As we step in deeper, Stevie brushes her fingers against the water trickling down the rock waterfalls and grins. "This is…" she pauses, trying to find the right word as her eyes circle around the room again.

"Nice?"

"Nice is an understatement." She says, looking up at me in disbelief. "This is just… wow."

I want to soak up the adoration in her eyes, even if it is for the fucking room. It's pathetic. But we came here to clean up her wounds, so I shake out of it and bring my focus back on her needs.

"Ready?" I ask, cocking my brow.

She gives me a quick nod and I carry her towards the sleek slate countertop. After carefully setting her me down, I take a few steps back and give her some space to undress.

Stevie continues to gape at the room. Studying every minute detail. From the large, glass encased shower to the live water plants the designer embedded into the rock walls.

I audibly clear my throat and give her a look.

"What?" She asks, cocking her head at the obvious question in my eyes.

I step forward and plant my arms on either side of her body. She shrinks back instinctively, and the predator within me roars to life. Slowly, I level my eyes on her and give her an appreciative stare.

Mere inches away from touching, she swallows and I breathe in her heady scent of rich vanilla and juicy pear. I can almost taste it on my tongue. The closeness is intoxicating.

"Can't exactly clean you with that on." I say, looking at Atlas' jacket, still swallowing her tiny shoulders.

"Oh." She replies, looking away as a flush creeps up her neck.

I try not to think about what caused it, but the mind is a cruel bastard. And with her nearly naked body so close to mine, it's hard not to think about sex.

Stevie fumbles over herself as she tries to shake off the jacket with a wince. She injured her palms almost as badly as she hurt her knees, so it's a feeble attempt. Instead of letting her go for a second try, I reach for the jacket and slide the silky black fabric down her shoulders myself.

Stevie visibly swallows and looks at me with pleading, come-fuck-me eyes as my thumb gently grazes her hot skin. My tongue swipes out to lick my bottom lip and her tongue instantly mirrors mine. My eyelids grow heavy and my jaw clenches. *Fucking hell.* She's making it damn near impossible not to think about sex.

Clearing my throat, I take a step back and turn my attention to the jetted tub. I start the water and grab a few supplies from one of the sleek glass cabinets adorning the walls.

"What's that?" She asks, studying me as I finish adding some oil into the water.

"T... tea tree oil." I offer, grabbing a few pads of gauze

and a tube of ointment from another cabinet. "It helps with the healing."

"You know a lot about treating wounds."

"Yeah." I say, releasing a heavy sigh. "This isn't the f... first time one of us has gotten hurt and I'm s... sure it won't be the last."

Hot, fragrant steam floats in the air as the warm water thunders into the tub. I turn towards Stevie and lift her into my arms again, doing what I can to avoid staring at her hot naked body as it jostles in my arm. I gently lower her in the steaming water and avert my eyes as she gets settled.

"The water's a little hot." I say, grabbing one of the black washcloths I stacked on the edge of the tub. "Let me know if it's uncomfortable and I can cool it down."

"It's fine." She says, eyeing me as I dip the washcloth into the soapy water. "What are you doing?"

"Cleaning you."

I gesture for her to turn around and she does so without protest. She slides her wet hair to the side and angles her bare shoulder towards me and turns to give me a seductive grin.

As soon as the warm wash cloth touches her skin, I feel the tension in her body dissipate. I work my way from the nape of her neck down to her shoulders, pressing deeper while simultaneously rubbing her muscles. I find an especially tight spot and when I squeeze, a tiny moan of relief escapes her lips.

For a split second, I freeze, and my cock painfully hardens.

Fucking hell.

"Lean back." I order, my voice rough and demanding. She

obliges almost immediately and stretches her body across the length of the tub.

Abandoning the washcloth, I move my bare hands towards her scalp and lather her hair with shampoo.

"It smells like you." She mumbles, her eyes still closed as I massage her scalp.

"I have a s... scent?"

"Mm hmm, like a mysterious forest. Grassy & woodsy, with a hint of something exotic."

I give her a grunt of a laugh and continue washing her hair. Her body is on full display and I'm having a hard fucking time staying a gentleman. With every move I make, the peaks of her nipples float above and below the surface of the water, calling to me like a fucking siren.

She releases another moan again, this time a little louder, and I watch her tongue flick out to moisten her bottom lip.

"Join me." She says, out of the blue.

My hands still and I stare at her for a beat to make sure I'm not imagining things.

"Hmm?"

"Craning my neck like this is a little hard," she says, blinking her eyes open, "it'll be easier if you're in here with me. Besides, there's plenty of room for the both of us."

It isn't the space I'm worried about.

FIVE

Stevie

I'M NOT SURE IF HE'S UNABLE TO ARGUE AGAINST MY reasoning or if he simply chooses not to. Either way, Tristan stands to his full height and strips off his clothes. It's not supposed to be a show, but his movements feel slow and seductive, as if time is moving differently.

Every pop of a button and every slide of a zipper reveals more and more ink coated skin and I can't help but marvel at the beauty that is Tristan's body. His golden skin is stretched tightly over powerful cords of muscle from the top of his thick shoulders to bottom of his muscular legs. His tattoos are placed with intention, highlighting the hard ridges of his chest and stomach and disappearing right before his mouth-watering v. His cock is perfect too, thick, long, and impossibly hard as it awaits my undivided attention. Tristan is a living god and I've never been more ready to praise him.

I push off the edge of the tub and glide backwards, giving him ample space to join me. The air in the room is fragrant, hot, and sticky, and when Tristan levels his emerald eyes on me, I can feel the heat rushing from the tip of my toes to the top of my head. I slink back deeper into the water, trying to disguise the hunger that's written all over my face. I've never craved this man so badly before.

Tristan steps into the water, and it's as if I'm watching a scene in a movie. The overhead light shines down on him, casting every single inch of his muscular physique in hard shadows and light. Even in his fully exposed state, he doesn't look vulnerable; he looks like he's headed into battle. His lips are set in a hard line, and his chiseled jaw is tilted up. Despite his closed off nature, nothing about this man is shy or timid. His movements are deliberate and his intentions are clear. Tristan wants to feast and I'm the only thing on the menu.

My eyelids grow heavy and my teeth sink into my bottom lip as he slowly inches his way towards me. Even the hot tendrils of steam can't seem to resist his charm. They rise from the water and swirl around him, almost as if they, too, were pulled in by his gravitational force. He sees my reaction and a sinister grin forms on his lips. He has me in the palm of his hands and he knows it.

Tristan sinks his head under the water and disappears, only to resurface within a hair's breadth away from me. Tiny beads of water trickle down the strong planes of his face, gliding off of his long, thick lashes and dribbling down his almost too full lips. His green eyes pin me with a primal stare and I know that neither of us can stop what's about to happen.

Our lips crash into each other in a violent collision. Tension, rage, and lust spill out between us as we lick, bite, and conquer each other's mouths with staggering force.

"You're a pain in the fucking ass." Tristan grunts, sinking his teeth into my bottom lip.

"So are you." I groan, fisting fingers full of his hair as I dive in for another violent kiss.

I feel his cock harden underneath me and I instinctively grind against him as if it's the most natural thing to do. Tristan pulls back and smirks, studying me as he dips his hand beneath us and opens the drain. *Last chance,* his eyes seem to say, as if I have any actual choice in the matter. I was fucked the second I asked him to join me. Now, there's no way in hell I'm stopping this now.

Our bodies mold against each other again in a tangle of limbs and slippery skin. The way we touch each other feels possessive, raw, and consuming. We needed this. This exchange of power. This battle of wills.

As the water plummets around us, I sink my hand beneath the shallow surface and wrap my fingers around his enormous cock. He's so hard and thick with need, and I can't wait any longer. I angle his cock towards my entrance and wince a little when the head breaks through. The stretch feels impossible, but I don't stop. I need to feel him pulse inside of me. I need to know that this is real. That everything happening between us isn't just a fever dream.

I pivot my hips slightly and lower myself on the full

length of his cock, soaking up the delicious pressure and fullness I feel as he slides all the way in. Tristan's head falls back, and he releases a rough groan as his large hands palm my ass. His fingers painfully grip my ass as he guides my hips up and down and up and down.

"Fuck, Baby. Just like that." He murmurs. "Just like that."

He leans my body forward and catches one of my nipples into his mouth, biting down with just the right pressure. He flicks his tongue against my nipple and my body jolts, sending a cocky smirk to his face. He does it again as he pumps into me and my head lulls. Loving my reaction, he picks up his tempo and does it again.

Flick and fuck. Flick and fuck. Flick and fuck.

We get into a rhythm that is so goddamn divine, so utterly earth-shattering that my body gives out and I become nothing more than a toy for Tristan to fuck.

He grips me tighter while his movements become more aggressive. Everything about the way he fucks me feels raw and primal. Like he is so maddened with lust, he could devolve into an animal at any moment.

He's gliding my pussy up and down his shaft faster now and the last remnants of water are splashing all over the place, but neither of us care. Our hunger has taken over.

He's fucking me harder, with pure abandon, and my bones are mush. I melt into him as he squeezes my ass and ruthlessly pounds into me.

Flesh against flesh. Heartbeat against heartbeat.

He grips my wet hair, tilts my head, and licks my throat from the base of my neck to the tip of my chin. "Mine." He grunts, thrusting harder. "All fucking mine."

I nod my head and mumble in agreement, knowing he

didn't expect an answer but giving him one, anyway. I can't even think straight. All I see is Tristan and all I feel is his cock as it mercilessly pounds into me.

"Moan for me." He groans, biting my neck in a rough, animalistic claim. "Let me hear that beautiful fucking voice."

And I do. I moan his name like I'm saying a prayer. Like he's a god and I'm worshiping at his altar. And he fucks me like I'm his goddess. Like this is his own personal way of honoring my divinity.

A powerful orgasm ricochets through me, and my eyes roll into the back of my head. Tristan's cock fills me up while simultaneously ripping me apart, and it is the best feeling I've ever had.

My pussy squeezes tightly around his cock and he fucks me harder and faster until his own climax has him groaning in rhythm with my moans. It's animalistic. It's primal. And it's fucking perfect.

After coming down from our impossible high, we finish cleaning up, dry off, and eventually pull ourselves out of the bathroom. Tristan carries me to my room and carefully dresses my wounds before crawling into bed beside me. We don't speak, but we don't really need to. Our bodies spoke for us.

I fight to keep my eyes open as we lay in bed, gazing into each other's eyes. His lids are heavy too, and I can tell that neither of us wants this night to end. I feel a closeness to him I've never felt before and I don't want anything to get in our way again. It's like we used to be two separate planets. Afraid to get too close to each other in fear that one's gravity will throw off the other's. But somehow, among all the chaos, we found a way to stay in each other's orbit and now, neither of us wants to leave.

I close my eyes, just for a moment, and breathe him in. The heady scent of a lush evergreen forest overtakes my senses and I let out a soft sigh. This is exactly where I want to be right now. With my silent protector. My breathing evens out and sleep slowly creeps in. I try to fight it, but every part of my body gets heavier and heavier with each passing moment.

"Stay?" I mumble, keeping my eyes closed. "Please." I hate how vulnerable I sound, but I need him with me tonight, now more than ever.

Tristan presses a soft kiss on my forehead and runs his thumb along my cheek. "I'm not going anywhere, Baby." He whispers. "You have my word."

And with that promise, I drift off to sleep and dream of a silent knight who helped me slay my dragons and was finally ready to put down his shield.

SIX

Atlas

I hear the sound of his Ducati roaring down the road seconds before his bike comes into view. I knew it was only a matter of time before he got word and as expected, Cyrus looks pissed. Staring at him from my second story office window, I watch as he dismounts his bike and quickly shoves his way towards the front entrance to Hell's Tavern. The smoking section out front is packed, but once they see who's barreling through, they quickly move out of his way.

The panoramic two-way mirror on the floor of my office

gives me a clear view of the entire club, and as I look down, I see Cyrus enter the building. Even from nearly thirty feet away, I can see the rage radiating off of his shoulders.

Every person he comes into contact with seems to sense it too, giving him a wide berth as he passes through the packed dance floor. It's just after 10pm and the crowd on the dance floor is just starting to get rowdier as the heavy bass thunders through the walls. Cy seems unfazed by it all as he shoves his way towards the staff-only door that leads to the second floor offices.

3... 2... 1...

"Atlas!" He booms, kicking the door off of its hinges. His boisterous voice echoes down the nearly empty corridors, making most of the startled staff scurry out of his way. "Show yourself, motherfucker!"

If he was blowing up over any other reason, I would've ended this tantrum before it even started. But in this case, Cy has every reason to be pissed and he just needs someone safe to let it out on.

It's the reason I chose not to tell him the news the second I found out. I knew the minute he got word, the first thing he'd do is come to me for an explanation, rather than doing something really fucking stupid.

Stepping out of my office, I reach the top of the stairwell just in time to see Cyrus pinning an unwitting security member against the wall.

"Where the fuck is he?" He spits, his chest rising and falling in rhythm with the vein pulsing in his neck.

Instead of answering, poor Victor just trembles under Cy's hold. Too scared shit-less to say or do anything. If he doesn't give Cyrus an answer, he's fucked, but he's equally as fucked if he discloses my location without my permission. Deciding to put the poor kid out of his misery, I speak up.

"Let 'em go Cy." I call out in a bored tone. "I'm the one you want, remember?"

Re-entering my office, I head straight for the wet bar and pour myself a shot of Macallan. I've been trying to avoid drinking, but the impending conversation with Cy warrants a glass or three. Timing it perfectly, Cyrus busts through the door of my office just as I take a seat behind my desk.

"I just want to know one thing." He spits, circling me like I'm his wounded prey. "When the fuck were you planning on telling us?"

"I haven't had the chance." I reply coolly, swirling the rich whiskey in my glass. "He showed up here, unannounced, an hour ago."

"Well he's sniffing around the docks as we speak, my boys over there shot me a text."

That's one of the major differences between Cy and I. With his charisma and easy charm, he makes friends wherever he goes. I may get respect from the power I hold, but Cy earns it, just by being the man he is.

"Where's Stevie?" I ask, only now realizing that he and Tristan were supposed to stay with her tonight.

At the mention of her name, the tension in his shoulders eases and the fire in his eyes wanes a fraction. After her little stunt earlier, the last thing any of us wants is for her to hurt herself again. It's why Ez insisted on retrieving her sister tonight. I wanted to send a crew with him but with Dimitri's sudden appearance, we needed all of our men on top of their shit tonight. Besides, how hard could finding an eighteen year old kid be?

"She's fine." Cyrus replies, taking the seat across from me. "Tristan's with her."

"What the hell is Dimitri doing here anyway?" He asks, his features scrunching into a scowl. "Los Angeles pussy no longer suiting his tastes?"

"Oleg died." I sigh, taking another slow sip. "Heart attack. Mitri came to deliver the news personally."

"Shit." He curses, running a hand through his hair. "I'm sorry, At. I had no idea."

At sixteen years old, Oleg saw potential in me that no one had. When we first met, I was a cocky little shit and after a few successful pickpockets, I thought I was untouchable. I spotted Oleg stepping out of an expensive Porsche with a smug smile that screamed old money. He wasn't a large man, easily under six feet and less than 200 lbs. His dark salt and pepper hair and the fine lines around his eyes gave me every indication that if we were to tousle, my youth would be a major advantage. I was big for my age, already over six feet and still growing into my gangly limbs.

Unable to resist the temptation of such an easy target, I stupidly tried to swipe the Rolex off his wrist in the middle of a busy downtown intersection. As soon as my fingers grazed the cool metal, I felt a strong hand clamp onto my shoulder and throw me to the ground with lightning fast reflexes. Within a blink of an eye, I had ten handguns pointing directly at my head and Oleg still had that smug smile on his face. Like he was amused by my fatal judgement call. Instead of killing my ass, like he had every right to, he called off his crew, spared my life, and gave me a new life.

Despite me not knowing shit about The Organization, Oleg took me into his home and taught me how to make something of myself. He knew I wanted to save my brothers and he taught me the skills necessary to provide for my family.

I worked my way up through the west coast ranks of The Organization for a couple years and once I ranked high enough, my brothers and I took control of Caspian Hills and never looked back. Without Oleg, there would be no Reapers. Oleg was the father we never had, or at least, the man who took over after ours was killed. I was going to miss the old bastard. We all were.

"Don't worry about it." I say, grateful the turn of the conversation managed to cool him down. "The last thing he'd want is any of us moping around mourning him."

"True." Cy offers with a solemn nod. "He was a stubborn bastard wasn't he? So, when are the services?"

"A week ago." I pause, taking a slow sip of my whisky and relishing in its burn. "Apparently Carolina wanted to limit the services to family only."

"That's bullshit."

I agree with him but the whole situation is out of our hands. Unlike her late husband, Carolina never considered me or my brothers her family. When I first met Oleg, he was still a bachelor, with a new woman in his bed every night. He enjoyed his single life to the fullest. Honestly, I never expected him to settle down and assumed that his bachelorhood was something ingrained in him. But after an extended trip to Moscow, he came back a completely changed man. He was head over heels in love with a new fiancee who, coincidentally, came with a new stepson for him to mentor.

My brothers and I tried to build a bond with Carolina but the harder we tried, the more she shut us out. Eventually we learned to stop trying altogether. She never outright said it, but I could tell it bothered her to know that Oleg treated me and my brothers more like his own than he ever did Dimitri.

"Too late to make it an issue now." I say, clenching my jaw. "Oleg is six feet underground as we speak."

"Alright." Cyrus says, nodding his head. "I'll give you some space. Listen, if I'm not around as much for the next few days…"

"Yeah I know." I reply, turning in my chair to gaze down at the panoramic glass. "It's for your own sanity."

"There's something else you should know." I say, hesitating as I turn back to face him.

Cyrus stands perfectly still, almost as if he already knows where this is going.

"He's Oleg's successor."

"Are you fucking kidding me?" He asks, disbelief marring his features. "And the council approved that shit?"

"They're the ones that selected him." I say, feeling the full weight of defeat pile on my shoulders. "Apparently Oleg never told them otherwise."

I would've been honored to take over for Oleg, but I knew being selected was a long shot. Oleg was sold, but he wasn't the only one with the power to make the decision.

"That's bullshit!" Cy says, rubbing his forehead. "Oleg never shut up about how he couldn't wait to see what you'd do as his successor."

"It doesn't surprise me. The Organization is still… *traditional* when it comes to putting men into a position of power. They still have their doubts about us."

"Because we aren't Russian." He hisses through gritted teeth. "Fucking assholes."

"It's fine. We're great at what we do. If we haven't proven our loyalty to them by now, we never will."

"You're right." He sighs, running a frustrated hand through his hair. "Still think it's a good idea to keep Stevie a secret from the rest of The Organization?"

"I do." I say, taking another slow sip. "Even more so now that Mitri's been promoted. As far as they're concerned, she is a friend that works at the club. Identifying her as anything else…"

"Will only make him want her more."

"Exactly. You out of all people know how detrimental that would be for all of us."

"Don't remind me." He says, pacing the floor. "So what do we do now?"

"We do whatever we can to make sure Stevie stays off of his radar and we wait for this little pissing contest of his to blow over. He wants to flaunt his power, so we let him. He'll get bored with the games and leave like he always does."

"And if he tries anything with Stevie?"

"Then we kill him." I say, leaning back into my leather seat. "There's always risks involved when stepping into such a powerful role. I'm sure The Organization has another pure-bred backup plan ready to go."

SEVEN

Stevie

THE SECOND MY SKIN TOUCHES THE COLD SHEETS NEXT TO ME, I know something's wrong. I open my eyes and wake up to an empty room cloaked in darkness. Tristan isn't here and probably hasn't been here for quite some time.

    I glance at the clock on my marble nightstand and do a double take. 12:17 AM. We fell asleep around 9:30 PM, which means he couldn't have slept for more than a couple of hours. Tristan promised that he'd stay with me tonight. Something must have happened for him to break that promise and leave like this. Something big.

Scrambling out of bed, I whip the black silk sheets to the floor, throw on an oversized band t-shirt, and march straight for the door. If something is going down, especially if that something involves my sister, I have to be there.

As soon as I grab the door handle and feel the resistance of the lock in place, my heart immediately sinks. The asshole locked me in. *Again.*

"Tristan!" I scream, slamming my balled fists against the wooden door. "Open the door!"

The pain in my palm kicks up, but I shake it off. I need to get out of here now.

"I know you're out there." I call out, getting more hysterical by the second. "Open the fuck up!"

Assuming he's outside is a hunch, but I know the guys. Even if something is going on, they'd never leave me completely unprotected. Hell, they didn't even leave me alone with their own staff.

I'm about to start another bout of yelling when I hear heavy footsteps approaching. Silence fills the air as unease creeps into my mind. *Shit, what if it isn't the guys?*

I instinctively step back as my heart thunders in my chest. *What if someone broke in and my dumb ass just put a huge target on my back? Stupid. Stupid. Stupid.*

Beep.

The second I hear the mechanical sound of the door unlocking, my worry instantly washes away. It *has* to be them. They're the only ones with access cards. They don't even give members of their own security team that kind of clearance.

Staff still use regular keys and are only allowed access to certain spaces on the estate.

Giving the door just enough space to open, I'm ready to give whoever it is a mouthful, but I nearly choke on my words as the door swings open.

My eyes bulge as a complete stranger strolls into my room. He isn't one of The Reapers, but that isn't what catches me so off guard. The man is monstrous. A few inches shy of Tristan and Cyrus in height, but at least 1.5x their mass. While The Reapers maintain lean muscular physiques akin to The Greek Gods, this man has the body of a barbarian. Thick cords of muscle fill out the fitted herringbone slacks he wears and as he cocks his head, his golden brown brushed-back hair gleams in the pale moonlight. He relaxes his sharp, bearded jaw as his soft blue eyes scan the entire room before landing on me.

"Who are you?" I ask, looking at him accusingly.

They would never leave a stranger alone in their house like this. Let alone give him an access card. *Who the hell is this guy?*

"I could ask you the same." He laughs with the tinge of a Russian accent. "I am many things for many people, but you can call me Dimitri."

"Dimitri." I say, drawing out his name as I cock a brow and assess him further.

He wears a freshly pressed white shirt that doesn't have a wrinkle in sight, a flashy diamond-encrusted Rolex watch on his wrist that's probably worth more than my old car, and a smug smirk on his golden tanned face that screams wealth and power. I'm not one to judge a book by its cover, but this man has Russian Mafia written all over him. Still, the question remains, is he a friend of The Reapers or a foe?

"Where are they?" I start, then almost immediately regret my question as soon as I see the hint of amusement in his blue eyes.

"Hmm." He murmurs, his deep voice sinking into my bones. "*They* have some business to attend to, though I doubt they'd keep such a lovely creature waiting long."

Despite his calm demeanor, something about his choice of words sets off warning bells in my head. Suddenly, I'm very aware of the fact that he and I are alone in this house and the only fabric covering my body is a thin white Aerosmith T-shirt.

"Oh, that's right." I say, dramatically slapping my forehead for emphasis. "Tristan mentioned he may have to work tonight. Thanks for opening the door, but I better get back to bed. He'd be so angry if I wandered off somewhere."

Tristan mentioned nothing to me, but I can spot a predator when I see one. And the way his blue eyes follow my every move terrifies me. My best bet is to play up the ditzy girl act and hope he doesn't see right through my bullshit. Tristan left me locked in here for a reason and I'm willing to bet that this asshole was it.

"Are you sure, Kroshka?" He asks, cocking his head with a strange glimmer in his blue eyes. "You seemed eager to escape only moments ago. Why the sudden change of heart?"

The swift change in his tone is jarring. One minute his voice is smooth, soothing even, but he coats the last question in ice. I try to remain calm, but there's an undeniable threat behind his words and panic settles in.

"It's okay, really." I say, flashing him a smile I don't feel as I move towards the door. "I just met him and I'd hate for him to think I was so dramatic the second he left. Could this just stay our little secret?"

Pretending I'm insignificant to Tristan is purely instinctive. Something about the way Dimitri stares tells me he is a very calculated man. It's no accident that he's here alone with me. He was snooping around the house because he knew no one would be here. Probably planned for it. He thought he was alone and now he's trying to figure out what he should do with me. My best bet is to pretend like I'm an insignificant dot on his radar. "That's disappointing." He muses, slowly advancing towards me. "You didn't strike me as a liar, Stevie Alexander. But I suppose looks can be very deceiving."

I rear back and look at him, completely puzzled. *How the hell does he know I'm lying? And more importantly, how does he know my name?*

"You should leave." I snap, forgoing the naïve act altogether. "Before you do something stupid."

He stares daggers at me as he moves towards the exit. Inch by inch, I feel myself reluctantly shrink beneath his gaze. He's just one man and I've faced much worse before, but his presence alone is terrifying.

Just before reaching the threshold, he pauses and leans into me. "I can smell your fear, Kroshka. Tell me, which is it that scares you most? That I'm still here, or that deep down, something within you doesn't want me to leave?"

Before I can do anything to stop him, he whips around, grabs me by my waist and slams my body against the door, shutting it closed in one swift motion. The shock of what he's doing and the sheer power behind his force muddles my mind, leaving me frozen in fear as he continues to speak.

"Don't be shy." He coaxes, pressing his hard cock into my stomach. "See? The feeling is very mutual. Look at what those deceitful lips have done to me and they aren't even wrapped around my cock yet."

His vulgar words shake me out of my stupor and my hand whips across his face and slaps his cheek with a loud crack.

"Get the fuck off of me." I hiss, trying to shove his large body away.

But Dimitri doesn't budge, and his smile only grows wider.

"We both know that's the last thing you want." He grins, gathering my wrists in one large hand while his free hand travels down my body.

I try to wiggle and jerk out of his hold, but the more I struggle, the wider his vicious smile grows. I spit and I kick and I stomp and I knee, but fighting him only seems to make him crush my wrists harder.

The second I feel a thick finger slip in between my legs, I want to cry. Not because of the violation, but because of the cocky smirk that spreads across his face the minute he touches the wetness seeping out of me.

"That's more like it." He coaxes, grazing his thumb against my sensitive clit as he slides another thick finger inside of me.

Despite hating every second of what he's doing, my treacherous body writhes under his touch and he watches with cruel amusement at the involuntary reactions I'm trying desperately to fight.

You feel nothing. You feel nothing.

The sadistic gleam in his eyes terrifies me. This isn't about my satisfaction. This is about proving a point. To who,

I'm not sure. As far as he knows, I'm The Reapers' girl, which means he knows how much shit he'll be in when they find out. The asshole is either suicidal, or he has some insane ulterior motive.

I block out every spasm and jolt his vile fingers pull out of me until a hate filled orgasm rips through me. He relentlessly rubs my over-sensitized nub, but I refuse to show it on my face, even as wetness seeps down my leg and involuntary tears stream down my cheeks.

It isn't until I feel his movements slow down that I know it's over. He got what he wanted. He didn't rape me, but with how disgusting I feel, he may as well have.

"All better?" He asks, smirking as he removes his fingers from my slick center and finally releases my wrists.

"Fuck you." I hiss, my voice coated in venom.

I throw a solid punch to his jaw and my fist slams into the flesh of his cheek with a loud crack. He's surprised by the hit and his head wildly jerks back before he's able to recover.

"In due time, Kroshka." He chuckles, rubbing his cheek as he moves me aside to open the door. "In due time."

I don't know what comes over me. I know I should stay quiet and cower away. I have no weapons, no real means to defend myself against this monster of a man, but all I can focus on is doing whatever I can to hurt him like he hurt me. To draw blood from that stupid, smug face of his.

"Hey!" I yell, chasing after him as he walks down the hallway. "We aren't done here asshole, not by a long shot."

I grab a hold of his elbow and jerk his gigantic body around to face me.

"They will find you, and when they do, you'll wish you never laid a single fucking finger on me."

Threatening him is irrational. He knew what he was doing and what the repercussions would be when he touched me, but I want to see his fear. I want him as terrified as I was.

"I know your men." He says, brushing me off of him. "Better than you ever will. Trust me, Kroshka, there will be no love lost. Not over a toy, like you."

"A toy?" I scoff, stepping in front of him to face him head on. "I'm a fucking person and I didn't ask for any of that."

"Refresh my memory." He says, eyeing me up and down with a clear look of disdain. "Did you ever tell me to stop?"

No.

"Did you ever say no?" He presses further.

No, again.

"My point precisely." He says, laughing at my silence. "You simply needed to say the word, but you didn't. That, my sweet girl, was your truth. You don't want to admit it, but your body craved my touch."

I stare up at him for a few moments, at a complete loss for words.

This man is a fucking sociopath. A literally fucking sociopath.

As he moves to step away, I etch every single detail of his face into my brain. I want to know, beyond any doubt, that I have the right man when I come for him. And I will come for him. Whoever this Dimitri asshole really is, he's a dead man.

"Before I forget," He says, stopping a few inches past me. "If I were you, I'd keep this brief encounter of ours quiet. The Reapers are a valuable asset to The Organization and I'd hate for something to happen to them because their confused little toy foolishly threw herself at their boss."

Their boss.

"Be sure to clean yourself up before your men get home." He says, flashing me a cocky smirk. "I'm sure those possessive bastards would hate to see how wet another man can make their toy."

And just like that, the rage within me boils over. I didn't want to give him the satisfaction of a reaction, but we're well beyond that now. How dare he threaten my men? How dare he insinuate that what he did was anything but assault? Dimitri foolishly thinks he can throw the weight of his position around and that it'll intimidate me, but newsflash asshole, I don't give a fuck what your job is. I'm not a part of The Organization and the only rules I abide by are my own.

I clench my fists so tightly they turn white. I've never been so enraged. Never felt so incredibly unhinged. If I had the power to, I would rip Dimitri apart limb by limb and he knows it. He stares at me again and for the first time, I see a glimmer of unease cross his face. *Good motherfucker, you should be scared.* I don't know how and I don't know when, but I know one thing: Dimitri will die. And I'll be the one smirking as he takes his final breath.

"We interrupting something?"

Cyrus.

At the sound of his voice, I freeze and shame flushes my cheeks almost immediately. I slowly turn around and come face to face with Tristan and Cyrus as they step onto the second floor landing. I know what it must look like to them. Even without a mirror in sight, I can tell my skin is flushed, my hair is mussed from trying to fight him off, and my knees are still wobbly from the orgasm he forced out of me.

"It's not-" I stammer, struggling to find the right words.

"Relax, Kroshka." Dimitri chastises, wrapping his arm

around my waist in a gesture that is anything but friendly. If they didn't already assume something happened, seeing his aggressive touch is the nail in the coffin. "The twins *love* sharing their toys. Isn't that right, boys?"

Cyrus only stares at us, his brows furrowed in a mixture of rage and disbelief.

"Of course." Tristan offers, his features smooth and his tone even. "What's ours is yours, brother."

Brother.

Rage boils in my blood and I can't decide what angers me more. That they left me here alone with a stranger and basically just gave him the green light to fuck me or that, according to Dimitri, I am just one of many woman they've shared with him.

"I trust you've already taken care of our little problem?" Dimitri asks, flashing them a toothy grin.

"Atlas is on it." Cyrus spits, his eyes solely focused on the hand still wrapped around my waist. "It wasn't a four-man job after all."

"What problem?" I ask, then almost immediately curse at myself for bringing the attention back to me.

A dark chuckle fills the room as Dimitri's features morph in delight. I'm doing a real shit job of staying unseen. I look at Cyrus and Tristan, but their expressions are as unreadable as ever. *What the fuck is going on?*

"So curious." Dimitri croons, patting my cheek. "Intriguing little thing, is she not?"

Cyrus scoffs and stares at me with pure disgust in his eyes.

"If you find that whole deer-in-the-headlights thing appealing."

Why are they acting this way? Had they sobered up after

everything that went down yesterday? Realized that being with me had caused them nothing but headache after headache.

"Yeah," Dimitri says, licking his lips as he looks my body up and down. "Very much so." If the twins notice Dimitri's blatant ogling, they don't show it. Instead, they focus their angry glares on me.

"What the f… fuck are you doing out of your cage, Pet?" Tristan asks, finally cocking his head in my direction. He says nothing else, but the bone-chilling look on his face speaks volumes. I'm terrified of the man glaring back at me, more scared than I ever thought I'd be. So scared that for a moment I forget he's actually waiting for me to answer him.

"I… I was looking for you." I hesitate, not wanting to dispel any information in front of Dimitri. "I thought something happened with that thing and I thought I could help."

Cyrus snaps out of his trance and the bitter laugh he barks out rattles my bones.

"You thought *you* could help?" Cyrus scoffs, glaring at me with so much bored disinterest that it hurts. "No offense, Pet, but we have actual business to attend to. So why don't you go back to your fucking crate like a good little toy and wait until we summon you."

I walk back to my room, too deflated and hurt to bother trying to hide it. The last thing I see before Cyrus slams the door in my face is the satisfied grin on Dimitri's brutish face as he mouths the words "Until next time… Pet."

EIGHT

Stevie

KNOCK. KNOCK. KNOCK.

I know who it is before either of them say a word. The second Dimitri's car peeled out of the driveway, I could hear the twins' heavy footsteps practically running towards my room. They're probably eager for answers. *So much for being alone with my thoughts tonight.*

The "business they needed to attend to", as Cyrus so eloquently put it, took a little over an hour. During that time, I cried, I screamed, and I cursed at the assholes I thought I loved. And though Atlas and Ezra weren't there, deep down, I know they would have treated me with the same careless disregard. It's what they do and who they are at their core.

I don't answer the knock, but it doesn't surprise me when I hear the handle move. The door glides open and a soft breeze brushes my hair back as the two massive men enter my room.

I'm trying to hide it, but I'm still so angry. So god damn mad, I can't even think straight. So I revert to what I know and let the numbness act as my shield. No one else is going to hurt me tonight, that I can fucking guarantee.

I'm seated in one of the white loveseats poised in front of the roaring gas fireplace with a copy of Crime and Punishment in my hands. How fitting that a house filled with murderers enjoys reading about one.

"Can I help you?" I ask, not even bothering to look up from the pages I'm pretending to read.

I can feel the weight of their stares on my skin and it makes me internally sneer. I'm sure they expect me to fight them. For me to demand an explanation the second they walk in. But this is what they want, right? For me to be a good little whore and stay in my fucking place. I'm giving them exactly what they asked for.

Tristan is the first to make a move. He shuffles forwards and quietly sits in the chair next to me. I do and say nothing. The floor is theirs.

He releases a heavy sigh and leans forward. "We need to t… talk." He says, his rough voice sounding almost as defeated as I feel.

"There's nothing to talk about." I say, soaking in the ice that coats my tongue.

They've already shown me how little I mean to them. They didn't give a fuck about what they walked in on earlier, so why even bother pretending to care now? What's there to be upset about, anyway? After all, Dimitri practically got their stamp of fucking approval.

I expected them to behave differently. To think and feel differently about me. But that, out of everything that took place tonight, was my biggest mistake of all. I should've known not to expect anything from The Reapers. Nothing can deter them from their cruel nature, and I was so fucking foolish to think otherwise.

Right now, all I care about is finding my sister and getting the fuck out of their home and out of their lives for good.

"Bullshit." Cyrus says, leaning on Tristan's arm rest. "There's a fuck-ton to talk about."

"Not really." I say, feeling as dead as I sound. "It's business, right?"

"Did he touch you?" Cyrus demands, jerking my chin up. I say nothing as I glare at him. Willing my eyes to look as empty as I feel.

"Did he fucking touch you?" He asks again, painfully gripping my jaw.

"Does it matter?" I say, blinking slowly. "You said it yourself, I'm a toy."

The way I emphasize the word makes his lip twitch. He's trying to put up the same icy shields as I am, but I'm better at it. I'm colder, and when it comes down to it, I can be more ruthless.

"Answer him." Tristan says calmly. "Please."

"Nothing happened." I say flatly with my face void of

emotion. "He opened the door, I stepped out, and you two walked up."

"That's it?" Tristan asks, studying my poker face.

"That's it." I say, glaring at him. They didn't need to know anything else. No one did. What happened with me and Dimitri will stay between him and I.

Nothing good can come from telling them what happened. They'll either brush it off and, in doing so, hurt my feelings even more or they'll overreact and end up getting themselves or someone else killed. I refuse to have any more blood on my hands. This battle is mine and mine alone.

"She's fucking lying." Cyrus says, glaring down at me. "I can see it all over her fucking face."

A laugh bubbles out of me.

"You're really going to accuse me of lying right now? After the way you two acted?"

"No." Tristan says, using his arm to push his twin back. "We're not."

"Is there anything else?" I ask the question as a formality, more than anything else. They won't get any genuine answers from me. Not anymore.

"Yeah, there is." Cyrus says, glaring his emerald eyes at me. "Put some fucking clothes on. Your sister is waiting for us."

NINE

Cyrus

"You're a f... fucking idiot, you know that."

Tristan's words bring a smile to my lips as I ease myself down into the armchair Stevie vacated. He was waiting for the opportunity to bite my head off and with Stevie finally out of earshot, now's his chance.

"Love you too, Bro." I say, giving him a playful wink as I stretch my arms along the back of the chair.

Tristan sits back in his matching chair and groans as he tilts his head back and closes his eyes. "What the f... fuck were you thinking?" He mumbles, trying to keep his voice down. Stevie may be out of earshot while she changes in her closet, but neither of us wants her privy to this conversation.

I glance at her closet door and mindlessly wonder what she'll come out in. After finding out she came to us with nothing more than a handful of shirts and jeans, the four of us made it a point to have our personal shoppers fill her closet with anything and everything she could need. We thought of asking Stevie for her input, but after seeing how she reacts to help of any kind, we decided it was easier for us to pick out the items ourselves.

"Hey, Asshole." Tristan whispers, kicking my loafer to get my attention and pull me out my head. "I asked you a question."

I turn back to him and give him a dismissive glance. "I was thinking we were about two seconds away from losing the only person any of us give a real shit about." I say, readjusting the watch on my wrist. "You saw the look on her face. She checked out."

Tristan releases a heavy sigh and rubs his palms down his face. He may hate what I did, but he knows I'm right.

As we sit in silence, I focus my attention on the gas fireplace and watch as the bright blue and orange flames dance wildly behind the glass. It's the only source of light in her room, and as the flames flicker around chaotically, I find myself more and more enthralled in their movements. The hypnotic trance I fall into bears a striking resemblance to how I feel when I watch Stevie. Like the flame, her movements can be wild and unpredictable, but in those moments of peace, where outside sources aren't pulling her in different directions, she's the most exquisite thing I've ever seen.

Tristan shifts forward in his chair and glares up at me. "You realize you're baiting her with s... something that isn't f... fucking real."

It could be real. We have no idea where her sister is, but that doesn't make it an outright lie. Ezra hasn't gotten back to any of us all night. So for all we know, she's in her room at the motel as we speak. "Drastic times..." I say, refusing to back pedal.

I don't regret my decision. As soon as I mentioned her sister, Stevie's eyes flickered back to life. Slowly at first, so slowly that I worried the things we said pushed her past the point of caring about us. But as soon as she started moving into action, I could see the old Stevie slowly resurfacing. Right now, she's warring within herself. Caught between wanting to kill us and wanting to thank us for bringing her to her sister. That is much better than how it stood between us only a few minutes ago. The way we treated her in front of Dimitri was necessary, albeit pretty fucked-up, but I'm hoping it isn't anything a little heart-felt reunion can't fix.

"What happens if s... she's not there, you dumbass?" Tristan grumbles. "Then what?"

I hadn't really thought that far. I just assumed Alex would come back to the motel once it got late. I mean, it's not like she has shit to do this late at night. She's a kid, for Christ's sake.

"Then we'll wait." I offer smoothly. Hell, I'll wait in that shitty motel parking lot for an eternity if it means Stevie will come back to us after the shit with Dimitri.

Dimitri should've never been alone in our home to begin with, and Tris has already deactivated all of our access cards to ensure the motherfucker won't be able to cross that line again. We still don't know how the hell he got a hold of one of our cards, but it's all too convenient that he shows up here the minute he knows we aren't home. Especially when he was the one who orchestrated the whole thing.

Apparently, Dimitri received an anonymous tip that one of our guys running the cocaine transition warehouse was skimming ounces off during transit. We wanted to wait until morning to deal with it, but Mitri offered for his team to handle it, giving us no choice but to go. If he was right, he'd use it against us to make it seem like our power was weakening and if he was wrong, he and his guys would probably pull some shady shit to make it seem like he was right.

Leaving her alone was the last thing any of us wanted to do, especially after almost losing her today. But he specifically requested for the three of us to be there. With Ezra MIA and Dimitri still trying to assert himself as the new head of west coast operations, we couldn't risk ignoring his demands. No matter how ludicrous they were. If we did, we'd feel the fucking fallout.

"Do you believe her?" I ask, glancing in Stevie's direction as she re-emerges from her closet on the other side of the room. "About Dimitri."

She takes a seat on her bed and pulls on the black ankle boots Tris picked out for her. She kept on the band shirt Ez chose and tucked it into the cutoff denim shorts I bought that show off her sun-kissed legs. The coat she picked out is Atlas' choice, an oversized black wool coat that hits just below her thigh. It's almost ironic. Even when she doesn't realize it, she's choosing a bit of all of us.

Tristan lets out a breath and sits back in his seat. "I honestly d... don't know what to believe. I want t... to."

I want to, too. If Dimitri so much as laid an unwanted finger on her, I don't know if I'd have it in me to stop from killing the bastard. Just seeing his vile hands wrapped around her soft waist was torture. All I could think about, all I could envision, was ripping his digits off and feeding them to the motherfucker one by one.

"Ready to go?"

The sound of Stevie's voice catches us both off guard and we quickly cut the conversation short. We'll table the Dimitri issue for now, but only because we have more pressing problems to tend to.

I jump to my feet and gesture for her to lead the way. "After you, Princess."

She steps out of the room and Tristan stands up to follow a few feet behind her. As he moves past me he pauses and levels a serious look at me. "You better pray we fucking deliver on everything you promised."

I've never been a religious man, but if there's ever been a time for me to pray for a miracle, it's now.

TEN

Cyrus

SILENCE FILLS THE DRIVE DOWN THROUGH THE CITY, BUT FOR once, it isn't an uncomfortable one. Tristan is too busy trying not to kill me for putting this whole thing into action, while Stevie isn't doing much of anything besides staring at the road ahead. She seems determined to get her sister, now more than ever. I just hope we aren't setting her up for another fucking disappointment.

We reach the business district, and Stevie's undeterred gaze on the road finally wanes. Her eyes flick up to the luxurious high rises surrounding us and she stares at them with a mixture of wonder and amusement in her eyes. She says nothing, but she doesn't need to. Her face says it all. She loves our city.

It's hard to picture Stevie's life before us. Living on the other side of town in a shitty two-story with an abusive meth-head stepfather. She's been out of that environment for weeks, but she still hasn't really gotten to see much outside of the walls of our home. It's the first time she's seeing Caspian Hills in all its glory and it's bittersweet to know that we're the ones who robbed her of seeing it for so long.

The air in Caspian Hills is cleaner, the roads are smoother, and the sidewalks are free of the trash and needles we all grew up around. It's everything Caspian Valley isn't, which is why my brothers and I set out to own this city so many years ago. It's clear that Stevie, too, has fallen under its spell.

Stevie rolls down her window and sticks her head out and smiles into the breeze. The action is charming as hell and as I stare at her through my own rolled-down window; I realize it's the first time I've ever seen her without a guarded expression on her face. She's fucking beautiful, so beautiful that I sit back and soak that shit up like it's the last time I'll ever see it.

Who knows, if shit goes south tonight, it just might be.

I fight the urge to smile as her long dark wavy locks reach into my window and whip against the skin on my face. The sensation feels familiar, but before I can fully place it, I'm taken back to a bitter memory. One I thought I buried a long time ago.

"NERVOUS?" *I ask, squeezing her closer to my body.*

Instead of answering, she stares up the driveway and visibly scowls. Her soft features distort into a grimace and a need to protect her fills my chest. All I want to do is throw her back on my Ducati and get her as far away from here as possible, but that would completely defeat the purpose. Besides, we've put this off for long enough.

The autumn wind stirs up again, carrying her emerald green dress with it. Her long brown tendrils gently whip across my face, enveloping me in a strawberry-scented cloud that makes my mouth water. Fuck, this girl, this fucking strawberry scented mythical being doesn't even realize how tightly she has me wrapped around her finger. How I'd do anything to make her happy.

"Let's get you inside, yeah?" I offer, rubbing her soft, bare shoulder.

"They're all in there?" She asks, glaring at the mansion in the distance.

"Well, since they all live here too, I'm going to assume yes." I say, gently turning her around to face me. "What's going on in that beautiful head of yours?"

She gives me a blank stare as her mouth opens and shuts, almost as if she's fighting the urge to speak.

"Nothing." She finally says, pressing her lips firmly together. "Just ready to get this over with."

She pulls out of my hold and sets off for the house on her own. It only takes a few long strides to catch up with her, and when I do, the icy glare she throws at me is almost enough to give me pause.

She isn't acting like herself. She hasn't been since we got here. But I know she's nervous, and mostly, I get it. There's a lot riding on this for both of us.

In the three short weeks I've known her, Hannah St. Clair has proven herself to be the most amazing girl I've ever met. Not only is she fucking stunning, but she's patient and kind. The calming ying to my bat-shit yang. As much as I didn't want to, I've fallen in love with her and it's about damn time I brought her home.

As soon as we enter the house, she stops in her tracks and pulls out her cellphone. She scrolls through her social media and shoots off a few lengthy text messages before she looks up at me again. She rolls her eyes at me and an involuntary flash of irritation crosses my face.

"What?" She snaps, noticing my scowl.

"Just expected you to be more present."

She's the first girl I've brought home. The first stranger any of us have allowed into our house. She knows how important this is to me. To us.

"I'm here aren't I?" She scoffs, crossing her arms across her chest as she cocks a brow at me. "You're the one that insisted I meet everyone before staying over. Excuse me if I'm not super excited to be interrogated by your psycho brothers."

Before I can respond, I hear footsteps approaching and decide to keep my mouth shut. She's nervous. This isn't like her.

My brothers appear in front of us within seconds, and by the stony look on each of their faces, I can tell they heard every word.

Trying to make the best of the awkward situation, I push her forward a little and break the uncomfortable silence.

"Everyone, this is Hannah." I say, offering them a shit-eating grin. "Hannah, this is everyone."

"Nice to meet you." She sneers, flashing them a mocking smile. "Is there a restroom I could use?"

"Of course." Atlas says, gesturing towards the staircase. "Upstairs. Third door on your right."

Hannah scurries away, and I'm faced with offering my brothers some kind of explanation for her shit attitude.

"She's nervous." I say, brushing a hand through my hair. "Give her a second to warm up and you'll understand why I brought her here."

I can tell none of them are buying the excuse, but they seem to let it slide. We make our way to the sectional positioned in front of the huge flat screen T.V. Tristan set up. The servers set out a lavish charcuterie board on the oversized walnut coffee table and the four of us decide to dig in while we wait for Hannah to come back.

"I have to say." Atlas says, clapping me on the back. "I never thought I'd see the day that you'd settle down, little brother."

I finish chewing my brie topped slice of baguette and grin.

"What can I say?" I say, shrugging my shoulders. "She's made me a changed man."

"Happy for you, bro." Tristan says, giving me a rare smile. "I'm just glad s... she let you out. Feels like we haven't s... seen you in weeks."

"Yeah, we've been a little busy-"

"What did you say her name was?" Ezra asks, cutting me off with an abrupt question. His brow furrows as if he's trying to search his mind for some long-lost memory.

"Hannah." I deadpan, cocking my head. "Why?"

"Where did you meet this girl again?" He asks, cocking a brow.

"Hell's Tavern... again, why?"

"So this beautiful stranger just strolls into our club and she has no idea who you are? You didn't find that at all strange?"

"What? No. I didn't. She just learned about everything last night."

Ezra gives Tristan a look and I can see the cogs turning in my twin's head. He whips out his cellphone and starts typing while I feel like the walls are closing in on me.

"What's with the fucking fifth degree?" I ask, confused by the sudden turn of events.

"I know that girl, Cy." Ezra says, nervously flicking his zippo open and shut. "I've 'seen' her before."

The way he emphasizes the word 'seen' is like a punch to the gut. By 'seen' he means fucked. Ezra fucked Hannah.

"That's impossible." I say, shaking my head so hard my vision blurs. "She isn't from here."

"Not here," he says, pausing as if he's debating whether he should reveal more, "at The Devil's Disciples' clubhouse in L.A."

The room feels suffocating and I shoot up from my seat to try to get more air into my lungs.

"She's a Haven girl?" Atlas asks, his features morphed in disbelief. His eyes flash back and forth between the two of us, almost as if he can't believe what's happening.

By Haven girl, he means the sex workers The Devil's Disciples hand-select to live beneath their clubhouse. Against Oleg and pretty much everyone at The Organization's wishes, The Devil's Disciples have been covertly dabbling in sex trafficking. It's all hearsay, but in a club under Dimitri Evanoff's leadership, I wouldn't expect anything less.

"No." I say, refusing to believe anything he's saying. "No fucking way. She's living at the fucking Ritz Carlton. How do you explain that?"

"You need to ask her s... some questions." Tristan says, clicking on the flat screen and switching to the security camera's live feed. *"S... starting with, what the fuck she's doing in Atlas' study?"*

After discovering the truth about Hannah, my brothers left me alone to deal with her. Instead of trying to catch her in the act, I decide to wait and see what she does next. There's nothing in Atlas' study that would be of any use to anyone anyway, and as I watch her take more pictures and send more texts, my anger only grows. How the hell could I have been so stupid? She was never my dream girl. She was just an intricate lie, constructed to hit me where it hurt.

I hear her delicate footsteps descending the stairs and I quickly shut-off the footage. I've seen more than enough.

"Where is everyone?" She asks, assessing the empty living room with a frown.

Rage licks across my skin, and it takes everything in me to stop myself from screaming at her. Like she gives a shit. I wanted to draw it out and lead her to a confession, but fuck it. Let's cut right to the chase.

"Who hired you?" I snarl, glaring at her through narrowed eyes.

"What?" She responds, blinking rapidly. "I don't have a job yet. I'm still getting settled in..."

I smirk and release a callous laugh. She wants to keep up the charade, huh? Well, fuck that. I'm in control now and she's about to see the side of me I always kept hidden from her. The part of me that helped solidify my reputation as one of the most ruthless assholes in this entire city. The Reaper is surfacing, and he's hungry for blood.

"Enough!" I demand, cutting her off. "You know what the fuck I'm talking about. Who. Hired. You."

Her eyes dart around the room like she's looking for a savior. Someone to come save her ass in the knick of time. Unfortunately for her, the only man that would've come to her rescue is me, and I have no intention of letting her deceitful ass go.

"I-I don't know what you're talking about." She says, slowly inching back towards the foyer.

She reeks of desperation and I smile to myself as her well thought-out facade falters. Sticky sweat coats her forehead and a vicious sneer overtakes her once beautiful face. I see her now, truly see her, and she's nowhere near as strong as I thought. Her fidgety hand reaches for her purse and I can't help but bark out another laugh at her pathetic attempt to call for help.

"Make another move and I'll kill you." I say, removing my gun from the hostler on my hip.

A tremor overtakes her body and I flash her a shit-eating grin as I level my gun at her chest.

"Y-you wouldn't." She says, shaking her head in denial. "You love me."

"No. I thought I loved you." I say bitterly. "Big fucking difference. Now tell me; who hired you?"

I cock my gun to prove my point. I don't need her answer. By now, Tristan has hacked into her cellphone and traced the numbers back to whichever asshole fucked with us. But something deranged inside of me wants to hear it come from her deceitful lips. I have my suspicions given our not-so-pleasant history with Dimitri, but we have to be sure before we make a move. The organization doesn't take intergang conflict lightly.

"He loves me." She screams. "If you harm a single hair on my fucking head, he'll kill you!"

The next few seconds happen so fast, my mind has a hard time keeping up.

Hannah lunges for my gun and, in the shock of our tousle, she manages to wrestle it out of my hold. I underestimated her. Just as I had during our entire relationship, and the irony of it all is a bitch.

I wasn't planning on spilling Hannah's blood tonight. I just wanted to hear the truth come from her fucking lips. I knew she was merely a puppet in the grand scheme of things, and the only one I really wanted to hurt was the master pulling her strings.

"You're so fucking pathetic." She says, barking out a wicked laugh as she levels my own gun on me. "Nothing like him."

Her once melodic laugh sounds putrid and wrong. It grinds against my bones and makes me grit my teeth as she continues to cackle.

"That may be." I admit, visibly swallowing. "But at least I'll die knowing the truth. Unlike you."

I'm baiting her, partly to prolong the inevitable and partly because she deserves to know the truth. There's no way I'm escaping death either way. We're standing too close to each other and my brothers are too far out of earshot to stop her. I signed my own death certificate the second I let her grab my gun.

Strangely, I've made my peace with my death. I made a mistake, and I trusted the wrong person. I put my brothers at *risk and brought a spy into our home. Dying tonight will be my penance for that.*

I level my eyes on Hannah and solemnly shake my head. She has no idea how fucked she truly is. The sad thing is, there's still a part of me that wants to protect her. That wants to shield her from pain at any cost. But that's not fair and goddamnit she deserves to know the truth.

"You're a pawn, Hannah." I say, willing her to hear the sincerity in my voice. "A means to hurt me and my brothers. Nothing more."

"That's not true." She says, her voice wavering slightly. "Mitri loves me."

Damn. The fucking bastard. Dimitri is using her own con against her and she doesn't even realize it. Yet even I can tell that her words have no real conviction behind them and it's clear she's trying to convince the both of us of their sincerity.

"Did he tell you we have security cameras?" I ask, nodding my head at the one pointed down on us.

She says nothing in response, but her frigid glare answers for her. He didn't.

"They're in every room in this house." I say, rotating in a slow circle. "Tell me, would someone who loves you send you straight into a trap?"

She narrows her eyes at me and blows her tousled brown hair out of her face.

"It wasn't a trap." She hisses, jerking the gun at me. "He sent me to gather intel. To take as many images as I could of Atlas' study."

I shake my head with a sad smile and can't help but feel sorry for her. I know what it's like to convince yourself that you're loved. I've been doing it my whole life.

"Dimitri knows there's nothing in there." I say, locking eyes with her. "He's been in our house countless times. Been left alone in that study on several occasions, and he's never once cared to look through our shit. Do you know why?"

She shakes her head no.

"Because he knows it would be suicide, love."

The 'love' part slips out, but somehow it still feels right coming out of my mouth. I loved Hannah. I know that with every fiber of my being. But she never loved me and that's the cold, harsh reality of Dimitri's wicked game.

Even as she shakily levels a loaded .45 at me, all I can feel is remorse for what's going to happen to her. Hannah will die tonight, one way or another. If my brothers don't kill her for killing me, Dimitri surely will. She served her purpose and he won't hesitate to dim the light in her beautiful blue eyes to clean up any evidence of his part in this whole mess. He'll win, and she and I will pay the ultimate price.

"Dimitri loves me…" She says weakly as tears trickle down her cheeks.

"I know, love. I know…"

I can't help but offer her comfort. Even though it's wrong. Even though she's the one who betrayed me. Even though she's going to kill me.

"He's going to kill me, isn't he?" She asks, looking up at me with so much clarity in her deep blue eyes that it crushes me.

"I'm sorry, Hannah."

"My name is Sarah." She says, blinking back tears with a sad smile. "Sarah Wilson, and for the record, I'm sorry too, Cyrus."

BANG.

I flinch my eyes shut the second the gunshot rings out and leap to the ground, but I know I'm too slow. Within seconds, I feel a warm, sticky substance pool around me, but I don't dare try to move. The coppery scent of blood stings my nose and I can't hear anything but the ringing in my ears. My body... Well, it's as if my body feels no pain at all.

Is this what death feels like?

It takes thirty long seconds for my brothers to find me. I count the seconds as I wait for death to come. Hannah is probably halfway to my Ducati by now. Probably shouldn't have given her a spare key, but hindsight is 20/20.

I feel their hands on me before I hear them enter the room. My ears are ringing and I have no idea what they're saying as they lift me up from the ground and begin trying to assess my wound. I'm surprised I can feel them, given my body's state, but I'm happy I get to see them one last time.

My brothers. My best friends. The only bastards in this entire world that understood me more than I understood myself. They'll survive without me, but I'll miss them like hell.

"Is he hit?" I hear Atlas ask, his voice booming through the ringing. "Is he fucking hit?"

I want to tell him I am; I have to be. She was the one with the gun. But I don't want to waste another second of my time talking. I just want to remember them.

"I d... don't know!" Tristan screams, as he frantically pulls at my blood-soaked clothes. Ezra pulls his pocket knife out and helps him cut the fabric loose, looking as unhinged as Atlas sounds.

Fuck.

If I knew I was going to die, I would've spent more time with them instead of chasing a girl I barely knew. Why is it only now that I realize just how important family is to me? When I'm on my fucking deathbed.

I glance to my left and search for Hannah, even though I know she's not there. I feel like a masochist, but I can't help but want to seek her out before I die. I loved her and even though she was the one who did this, in these last few moments of my life, I want to pretend like everything we had wasn't a lie. That she loved me and that she wasn't just a pawn in Dimitri's sick little game.

As I suspected, she's nowhere in sight. I'm sure she thought running was her best option, and I'm not sure I could've convinced her otherwise.

Dimitri is notorious for taking pleasure in tying up loose ends and, unfortunately for her, she is now one of them. Poor naive girl. My brothers would've at least had the decency to make her death quick. Dimitri will chase her, torture her for the fun of it, and relish in every second of her pain. He may look like Oleg's golden child, but he's a wolf in sheep's clothing, always has been, always will be.

My head falls down and I notice a flash of emerald green in my peripheral vision.

Hannah?

Jerking my head up, I blink my eyes rapidly, just to make sure I'm not hallucinating.

Hannah is lying in a pool of blood with her delicate fingers still wrapped around my gun, but her blue eyes are lifeless.

FUCK.

"Put me down." *I mumble as icy numbness takes over my whole body. This can't be happening. It was supposed to be me. It was supposed to fucking be me!*

All three of my brothers freeze and scowl down at me. Their faces express a kaleidoscope of emotions as they wait for me to clarify.

"I said put me the fuck down!" I yell, shoving their hands off of me.

I fall to the ground and crawl to Hannah's side. A wave of emotions batter against me as I stare at her lifeless body.

She betrayed me.

Gained my trust only to steal our power.

I should hate her with every fiber of my being. But I can't. I still love her and the pain of losing her is ripping me apart.

She was right. I wouldn't have pulled the trigger. I couldn't live with myself if I killed her. But she killed herself, and somehow that hurts more.

"Cy, you've been shot." Atlas cautiously points out. "We need to get you medical attention."

"It's not my fucking blood…" I say bitterly, rubbing tears away with the back of my hand. "It's hers."

All three of them go pale. They don't know what to say and I don't blame them. She was our enemy, but she was also so much more to me.

"Please, just get the fuck out of here, okay?" I ask, my voice cracking with emotion as I brush her blood-caked hair away from her face. "She may not have loved me, but I loved her and that's all that fucking matters."

"Cyrus."

"CYRUS." Stevie calls out again, her concerned brown eyes pulling me out of my reverie. "How long ago did the clerk see Alex go in?"

Shit. The only way to get Stevie's buy in was to make it more believable by embellishing the truth. Looks like I'll be digging that grave of betrayal even deeper.

"Less than an hour ago." I lie, keeping my face blank.

"That's good." She says, biting into her lower lip. "That means she'll definitely be there still."

She folds and unfolds her anxious fingers in her lap as her soulful brown eyes study the road ahead. Thick dense fog coats the hills, but the hazy moon peeks through breaks in the mist, streaking pale blue light across her face. She's beautiful, no doubt. But her resilience sets her apart.

The bullshit with Dimitri was a necessary evil, but I won't let him come between us again. Knowing him, he probably underestimates our girl. Hell, once upon a time, we all did. But if he thinks he can fuck with her to get to us, his own inflated ego will be his demise. Stevie is nothing like Hannah. She's strong, she's dangerous, and she's no one's fucking puppet.

ELEVEN

The drive through the city flies by and before I know it, the landscape in front of us changes. The tall skyscrapers of Downtown transform into the Valley's familiar corner stores and run-down gas stations, but soon enough, we pass those in a blur.

It's nearly 1am and as we cross the border into Oakville, there isn't a single car on the road besides us. Oakville is a quiet town with a whopping population of 1,304. Their downtown area, if you could even call it that, boasts ten 'mom and pop' shops and what I can only describe as the tiniest movie theatre on the planet. As we drive through, I'm not surprised to find the streets completely deserted and the handful of shops closed for the night. The city itself is so tiny that if you blink, you may miss it.

Tristan pulls the car to a stop in front of the town's lone red light and drums his thumbs against the steering wheel. Time ticks by slowly as we wait for the green light, and I can feel the adrenaline building within me.

We're less than ten minutes away from Dina's, which means we're less than ten minutes away from seeing my sister. Ten minutes away from reuniting with the only person in this world that loves me unconditionally. I used to count The Reapers in that same boat, but after what happened with Dimitri, I see where their loyalty lies.

I'm not stupid. I know this impromptu recon mission is a ploy to get themselves back in my good graces. And it could have worked if things had played out differently tonight. But I'm not sure if things can ever be the same with us again.

Right now, I'll play the part of the grateful girlfriend if it means I get my sister back. I don't know where Alex and I will go from here, but once I have her by my side, we'll figure it out.

An ear-piercing siren blares into the quiet night, penetrating through the glass windows and jarring the three of us into high-alert.

"Where is that coming from?" I ask, searching out into the darkness.

The bulky industrial buildings lining the street ahead block most of the view, but the siren seems to get closer.

"No idea." Tristan says, checking his mirrors as his hands

squeeze the steering wheel. "Wherever it's going, it's moving f... fast."

"I don't see anything." Cyrus adds, shuffling into the middle of the back seat. "It's probably heading back to the Valley."

"Yeah." I agree, hesitantly. "You're probably right."

We still see no sights of the source as the sirens simmer down to a gentle whisper in the distance. It's quiet again, but I still can't shake the feeling of foreboding the siren stirred up. Maybe it's my nerves, maybe it's my own pessimistic viewpoint, but something about tonight just doesn't feel right.

A few minutes later, we turn onto Dina's block and it feels eerily like the night I left Alex here. Darkness coats the sky and the streets virtually empty. All I can hear is the sound of my pounding heartbeat as Tristan drags the car forward.

The red glow on Tristan's knuckles is my first sign something's wrong. I drag my eyes up to his face and see the same eerie light radiating off of him. Crimson flashes across the planes of his chiseled face, highlighting his strong cheekbones in a soft pink while emphasizing the shadows in a darker shade of rust. His expression is hard to decipher, a mixture of confusion and concern hardens his stare.

I turn to see what he's looking at and my mouth falls open as chaos erupts around us. My stomach sinks as we watch a stream of people come shuffling past us. All of them look out of sorts. Some are crying and others look so terrified it steals my breath away.

"What the fuck is going on?" I ask, my voice trembling as I study each face that passes us.

"I don't know." Tristan answers honestly. "But we're about to f... find out."

Two parked cop cars block us from entering any further, so Tristan throws the car into park in the middle of the street, and kills the engine. He and Cyrus pull me out of the car as a unit, careful to keep their eyes on the strangers rushing past us. They flank my sides, acting as a barrier of protection as we wade against the sea of panic.

"Do you smell that?" Cyrus asks, glaring over my head at his twin. Tristan gives him a firm nod before answering.

"S… smoke."

Picking up our pace, the three of us rush towards the motel. Bodies collide with ours as our steps gain momentum, but the twins are like an impenetrable shield, and we move through the crowd quickly.

We round the corner of the building and the scene we find in front of us knocks the wind out of me.

Bodies.

At least a dozen littered across the parking lot. Some of them are still conscious with paramedics doing everything they can to help as their mouths scream in agony and their faces twist in pain, but most of them are lifeless. Nothing more than piles of raw skin and charred bones. A raging fire burns bright behind them, swallowing the old decrepit building with a startling quickness.

Cyrus immediately seeks the fire marshal and pulls him aside, discreetly sliding him a few bills for his time. Tristan does the same with a few of the police officers on scene, doing what he can to get as much information as possible. I'm frozen in place as I look out at the scene before me. I've never seen this much damage. This much brutal carnage. *How the fuck did this happen?*

Numbly, I duck under the caution tape and begin scanning

the bodies for signs of my sister. I'm doing my best to keep my emotions under lock, but it's hard not to be affected with so much devastation surrounding you. Everything in my gut is telling me she's not one of them, but I have to be sure and with no one around to stop me, this may be my only chance to see for myself.

The scent of charred flesh and burnt hair fills my lungs as I stop by each body. I gently slide the white sheets down and assess their features before carefully pulling them back up. Their faces are charred, some of them burnt beyond recognition, but none of them are even close to looking like Alex. Once I finish with examining the last body, I release a shaky breath and signal the twins. She isn't in the parking lot, but that doesn't mean we're in the clear.

I spot room 132 and my feet start moving towards the door of their own volition. At first, my steps are clumsy and unsure, but once I get my bearings, they turn into powerful and determined strides. A firefighter who takes notice of my path, tries to intervene, but my body easily slips out of his hold. I have to know she got out and I need to see it with my own eyes.

Ignoring the protests of the firefighters and medics on the scene, I dash for the doorway and throw myself straight into the burnt room. The fire already tore through this side of the building and I don't give a fuck if it isn't structurally safe. If Alex is in there somewhere, I'm not leaving her behind.

As soon as I get a good look around the room, I freeze. Everything is burned beyond recognition, but that isn't what rattles me. There, on her bathroom mirror in giant crimson letters, is a message. One that feels personal.

IT'S NEVER A CRIME TO STEAL FROM A THIEF.

In an instant, all the air in my lungs leaves my body. My world feels like it's spinning and my breathing becomes ragged. I try to find my balance, but my shaky knees give out from underneath me and I crumple into the singed carpet.

This was no freak accident.

This was a targeted attack.

And there's only one person I know that has the power to pull off something of this magnitude. The only person left who has something to gain by hurting me.

Melanie fucking Diaz.

TWELVE

Stevie

THE THREE OF US STORM INTO HELL'S TAVERN WITH ONE thing on our minds... finding Atlas and Ezra. As soon as we step through the front entrance, we see the club is raging, with a large crowd of sweaty bodies grinding on the dance floor. Electronic music is pumping through the speakers, and the hypnotic red lights only add to the seductive ambiance oozing from wall to wall. There's only thirty minutes left until closing, but by the way the crowd is behaving, you wouldn't know it. The bar is just as packed as the dance floor, and the bartenders are doing what they can to push out as many drinks as possible.

Hell's Tavern is loud, chaotic, and honestly it's the last place I want to be right now. But after trying to get a hold of Atlas and Ezra for the last thirty minutes with no luck, coming here was our only actual option.

The lighting in Hell's Tavern is so abysmal, I can barely make out the twins as they guide me through the dance floor. I try to search the crowd for Atlas and Ezra, but the flashing strobe lights make it nearly impossible to decipher anyone's features.

"We're never going to find them like this." I shout, my voice barely carrying above the thundering bass.

Tristan lets out a high-pitched whistle, and the DJ's head instantly snaps up. Tris gestures for him to cut the track, and within seconds, the music comes to an abrupt halt. The drunken crowd immediately goes into an uproar, but before it can escalate any further, Cy steps up on the stage and gathers everyone's attention.

"Listen up!" He booms over the sizable crowd. "We're closing early tonight. Everybody out. Now!"

As soon as the crowd recognizes who's making the call, they waste no time at all. They charge out of the building in such a rush, you'd think Cy just lit the place on fire. Even the drunk assholes sober up enough to join the evacuating crowd, deciding to wait outside for their Ubers.

As the last few stragglers trickle out of the front entrance, a slow clap starts from somewhere in the darkness. The twins quickly form a barricade around me and the three of us circle around the center of the room, searching for the source.

The search doesn't take long. Before we make a move, a

large silhouette emerges from one of the dark corners of the bar and steps forward into the light.

"Nice performance." Dimitri says, cocking his head with amusement. "If I may ask, what's the special occasion?"

None of your fucking business.

"Just looking f... for our brothers." Tristan says, keeping his face neutral. "You haven't s... seen them, have you?"

Dimitri shrugs his shoulders as he swirls the drink in his hand. Little beads of precipitation flick off and fall to the ground as the rich, coral liquid sloshes around the glass.

"Your guess is as good as mine." He responds, slinging back the rest of his hellhound in one gulp. He places his glass back on the bar and then slowly levels his eyes on me. "Kroshka," he says, licking the remnants of grapefruit juice from his lips, "care for a drink?"

"I'm good." I hiss, stepping closer to the twins. I haven't forgiven them, not by a long shot, but I need to set aside my feelings for Alex's sake. Every minute she's gone is critical and we're wasting time entertaining Dimitri's stupid questions.

"We said, 'everybody out'." Cyrus hisses through gritted teeth. "That includes you."

The words are friendly, but the way he delivers them is anything but. He gives Dimitri a hard glare, but the stubborn asshole just looks back at Cyrus with bored disinterest.

Instead of being thrown off by Dimitri's blatant disrespect, Cyrus shakes his head and smirks, almost as if he was hoping for that reaction all along. Cyrus advances towards him. His movements are predatory and his gaze is cold, like a hunter who's about to corner his prey after a long chase.

I see a challenge in Dimitri's eyes as he stares back at him.

Like he's just begging him to come closer. There's so much more to The Reapers' relationship with Dimitri than I thought. The tension between these two alone is staggering. I have no doubt in my mind that they'd kill each other if we let them. But before it can escalate any further, Tristan places a hand on his twin's shoulder and stops him in his tracks.

"It's a private f... family meeting." Tristan offers, staring at Dimitri with a stiff smile. "You understand."

Dimitri nods his head with a small chuckle and sets his empty glass on the bar top.

"Of course." He says, turning his large body towards the exit. "Gentlemen, it's been fun and Kroshka," he pauses, looking at me in a way that is anything but friendly, "I hope you have very sweet dreams tonight."

I really fucking hate that guy.

After brushing off Dimitri's useless distraction, the three of us bolt for Atlas' office and find the door locked. Tristan tries to knock, but when we don't get an immediate answer, the twins decide to kick the door in. After about five tries, the door finally flies off of its hinges and the dust clears just in time for us to see Atlas jerk himself awake. Even half awake, his survival instincts kick in. Without hesitating, he pulls out his gun and levels it at us with deadly precision.

"Down boy." Cyrus says, reaching out to lower Atlas' gun. "It's just us."

"What the hell are you guys doing here?" He asks, rubbing his tired eyes into focus. "I thought we agreed you'd stay with her at the house?"

The twins hesitate, as if deciding how to even begin describing the events of the evening. Hell, it would be hard for anyone to describe that much horror, but we don't have time to waste. Not when Alex's life is in jeopardy. So I say the first words that come to my head.

"We have a fucking problem."

I RELUCTANTLY PLOP down into the center of the black chesterfield and cross my arms over my chest. As soon as I explained my thoughts on what we found, Atlas said he needed a second to think. But really, what the hell is there to think about?

Its obvious Melanie took her. She's the only person on the planet who A. knew about my sister and B. would think I stole from her. Case fucking closed. Unfortunately, it seems as if I'm the only one who's convinced of her guilt. When Atlas asked, Tristan and Cyrus both hesitated to back my theory, saying we needed to look at every possibility before jumping to conclusions. *Fucking cowards.*

I shoot a hard glare at the twins, but they're too busy watching Atlas slowly pace back and forth to notice.

His office smells like him. Like expensive cologne and refined taste. Every detail in the room suits him. The furniture is modern and the walls are decorated tastefully, but what's even more impressive is the bird's-eye view the office provides. With his two-way mirrored floor, he's able to see the entire club from this room. No wonder he felt comfortable crashing here. That view, combined with the security teams, and the three deadbolts the twins had to kick-in to get through, would make anyone feel comfortable enough to sleep like a baby.

My exhausted body would love nothing more than to hide in a haven like this. To slow down and rest for just a few minutes. But I can't, because for every second I sit here, it's another second Alex could be getting hurt.

"You're being awfully quiet." Atlas notes as he takes a seat next to me.

"You guys won't listen either way." I mumble, picking at the stray denim strands on my cut-off shorts. "Figured I'd just save my breath."

"We're trying." He responds. "But what you're suggesting..."

"It doesn't make sense, P." Cyrus says flatly.

"Really?" I ask, glaring daggers at the three of them. "It's never a crime to steal from a thief? Tell me, who else would think I stole from them?"

"Jessie." Tristan points out, leaning against the desk as he crosses his legs.

The thought of Jessie having something to do with this hadn't even crossed my mind, but now that he mentions it, she too could've done something like this.

"No." Atlas says with a dismissive wave of his hand. "She's locked up. Besides, she wouldn't have the power to orchestrate something this complex."

"Then if it's not her, it has to be Melanie." I say, looking at Atlas with pleading eyes. "She's the only one who knows about Alex. She thinks I stole you. Taking my sister is her way of getting back at me."

Atlas' face contorts into a scowl.

"We still shouldn't jump to conclusions." He says, slowly

shaking his head. "We did last time, and it almost killed you."

"It could be your stepfather." Cyrus offers. "He's used her as a bargaining chip before."

"Or s… someone who knows what we did to your ex and his friends." Tristan adds, looking at me pointedly.

Shit. My list of enemies got a hell of a lot longer since the last time I checked it. Still, my gut is telling me that this whole thing has Melanie written all over it.

"It's Melanie." I say, shooting up from my seat as my body refuses to sit idly. I pace back and forth in front of the coffee table for a moment before continuing. "It has to be. We have to stop her before she hurts Alex."

"It's nearly 3am."

"You think she cares that it's 3am? She probably has her men fucking torturing my sister right now. If you don't want to take me, that's fine. I'll go by myself. I'm getting my sister back tonight. With or without you."

The room fills with silence as Atlas, Tristan, and Cyrus simply stare at me for a few beats. I feel a significant change happening within me and I think they can sense it, too. Before tonight, I always warred within myself. Fighting between doing right by Alex and doing right by The Reapers. But after everything that's happened, I can't continue fighting with myself. I've got to pick a side once and for all.

"Your idle threats are getting ridiculous, don't you think?" Ezra calls out, stepping into the doorway to join us. "You have no car. No money. Face it, Angel, you need us."

I eye Ezra as he slowly saunters into the office. He's shirtless and freshly showered, with a hint of soap still lingering on his skin. It's strange that there's a shower in here somewhere, but it makes sense given the activities that go on in the dungeon.

His black joggers are slung low on his hips, leaving his ink-kissed chest and abs on full display. He casually rubs a black towel through his wet hair and stares at the four of us with a question behind his eyes.

"What did I miss?" He asks, tossing the towel over his muscular shoulder.

"Stevie's sister has been taken." Atlas informs him as he runs a hand through his hair.

"And they left this at the s... scene." Tristan adds, showing Ezra the picture of the hand-written message.

"The plot thickens." Ezra says, leveling his eyes at me as he slides the phone back to Tristan.

"This isn't a fucking joke." I clip, cocking my head in his direction. "She's in danger."

Ezra scoffs as he slowly advances towards me.

"I'm aware." He deadpans as he towers over me. "But personally, I could give two shits about your sister. Why is any of this a concern for us?"

His careless disregard for Alex's safety pisses me off. I want to tell him to fuck-off, to leave if he doesn't want to help, but I can't give him the satisfaction. I won't.

Being cruel and heartless is just part of who he is. It's part of who they all are, really. They aren't men who will hold me close and tell me everything will be okay. They're men that will challenge me and push me in ways I never see coming. They'll break me over and over again, just because they can. The only way I'll ever be able to survive in their world is to beat them at their own games. To fight their cruelty with a brand of my own.

"You know what." I hiss, scanning his face like I'm trying to memorize every inch of it. "I'm going to let your casual disregard for my sister slide, because I know that, unlike your brothers, you're damaged beyond repair. But just so we're clear, you should be concerned. Alex was the only thing tying me to this city and without her, I'm as good as fucking gone."

I stand there quietly, studying his hard features. His dark, wet hair falls into his face as his smoldering dark grey eyes hold my gaze. There's so much unfiltered rage flickering behind his eyes that standing so close to him kicks my survival instinct into overdrive. Deep down, I want nothing more than to take back everything I said and tell him the truth. That I need him and even if I wanted to, there's no way in hell I could ever leave. That despite what he thinks about himself, he's still redeemable. But that's not how things work with Ezra. He can't accept my love, and if I approach him in a loving way, he'll see me as weak and I'll never earn his respect. I have to fight his fire with my own and inflict pain to battle the pain he inflicts on me.

"Look, I'm tired of fighting." I say, backing away from Ezra so I can turn and face all of them. "I just need to know. Are you guys coming with me or not?"

As soon as I'm done speaking, Ezra storms off in a blaze of white-hot fury. I want to chase after him, but after what I said, I'm probably the last person he needs to see right now.

I wait for a decision while Atlas, Tristan, and Cyrus whisper among each other. After a few minutes, they break apart and Atlas steps forward.

"There's no way in hell you're going without us." He says, his voice taking on an authoritative tone. "That you'd even think that shows you're not in the right headspace. We'll head there tomorrow." He continues, giving me a hard glare when I roll my eyes at him. "We need sleep and you need to calm the fuck down. If you attack her unprovoked in her own home, there's nothing we can do to protect you."

As much as I hate to admit it, I know Atlas is right. If we were to head to Melanie's right now, I wouldn't be able to stop myself from pouncing on her. I need time to calm down, if not for my sake, for Alex's.

"Fine." I say dismissively, crossing my arms over my chest. "Tomorrow then. Let's just hope Alex is still breathing when we get there."

"She'll be fine!" The twins assert in union, cutting their eyes at me.

"She's their only bargaining chip." Cyrus adds. "Whoever took her won't do anything stupid to fuck it up."

The three of them continue to talk about strategies for tomorrow's visit, but after a while, I stop listening. They say my sister's safe and every single part of me hopes that they're right. Not just for her sake, but for ours, too. If something happens to her, I don't think I'll ever be able to forgive them.

THIRTEEN

Stevie

As Cyrus, Tristan, Atlas, and I load up into Cyrus' Jeep Wrangler, I try not to think about Ezra's absence. He knew what time we were leaving for Melanie's, but when I knocked on his door this morning to retrieve him, I found his bed noticeably cold. I expected things to blow over overnight, but maybe the things I said pushed him too far. Calling him damaged beyond repair is one of the many mistakes I've made so far.

This morning, instead of using the time to catch up on

sleep like the others, I spent most of my time thinking about Al and those mistakes that led us here. The guys were right. I needed to get a hold of myself, to rein my emotions back in before I faced Melanie. But in order to do that, I needed to let myself feel them. Even if just for a moment.

So at 4am this morning, cloaked in the darkness of my room, I allowed myself a moment of weakness. One last time to wallow in all the fucking mistakes I made. To feel all the pain, hurt, and sadness I've been trying so hard to suppress. To cry until there were no more tears left to fall.

In a lot of ways, everything that happened last night still feels like a dream. Like some crazy ass twisted nightmare I can't seem to find my way out of. But when I close my eyes, I can still feel Dimitri's fingers digging into my wrists. And even after a long hot shower, the scent of charred flesh still lingers on my skin.

Yesterday was hell, in more ways than one. But today's a new day, and I'm determined more than ever to get my sister back.

The plan the guys came up with is simple. Whoever took Alex doesn't know we know she's gone yet. Which means, if it was Melanie, showing up at her house out of the blue like this could be our last opportunity to catch her off guard. To distract her long enough to hack into her phone and see if she had anything to do with it.

It's a fool-proof plan. At least, it will be if I can keep my emotions in check.

In the hours since Alex's kidnapping, my hate towards Melanie has only grown. Before all this, I didn't know shit about her. She was just a woman who hated me because of Atlas. But taking my sister makes it personal. This isn't some bullshit rivalry over a man. Alex is my family, and I trusted Melanie, or at the very least, I started to.

I know she has something to do with this, and I'd love nothing more than to beat the information out of her. But if I want the truth, I have to play nice. I'm not letting my hate for her fuck up what could be our only chance of getting my sister back.

ATLAS PULLS the SUV to a slow stop in front of Melanie's entrance gate and rolls down his window. On the drive up here, I realized just how stupid my whole "I'll go by myself" idea actually was. The place is like Fort Knox. There's a monstrous 12ft wall wrapped around the entire perimeter and, as if that wasn't enough of a deterrent, I've spotted at least ten different armed guards walking the property line in the last five minutes. There's no way in hell anyone is getting into her home without a written invitation.

A young man in a guard's uniform steps out of the guard station and approaches us. Even hidden under his navy baseball cap, I can tell he looks young. 19, 20 maybe. He levels his eyes on our car and as soon as he spots Atlas in the driver's seat, recognition flickers across his face almost immediately.

"Good afternoon, Mr. Cole." He says, reaching through the window to shake Atlas' hand. "New car?"

"My brother's." Atlas says, nodding his head towards

Cyrus in the passenger seat. Cy gives the guard a small wave and his friendliest smile, and the kid visibly relaxes.

"Let me get you two all checked in and you'll be on your way." He glances down at his tablet, pulls up what looks like a calendar, and begins scrolling through it. After a few swipes, his smile falters and his dusty blonde brow furrows in confusion. "It doesn't look like Ms. Diaz is expecting any visitors today."

"It's a bit of a surprise visit." Atlas confesses, keeping the calm smile plastered on his face. "I can call her for you, if you'd like? But that may ruin the surprise."

The guard hesitates, trying to decide between following protocol and not doing anything to piss off his boss. It's obvious Mel runs a tight ship, and he's having a hard time deciding which risk is worth taking.

"You know what, don't worry about it." He caves, setting his tablet down. "I'm sure it'll be fine. You can just buzz her at the front door."

"Thanks Tim," Atlas retorts, throwing the car into drive. "I appreciate it."

"Of course, Mr. Cole." Tim says, nodding his head. "Have a good day!"

As Tim rushes to open the gate for us, Atlas rolls up his window and firmly wraps his fingers around the steering wheel. He flashes Tim one last easy smile before we glide past him and enter through the gates.

"That was easy." Cyrus notes.

"Almost too easy." Tristan says peering up at the house suspiciously.

"Perks of being her fiancé?" I muse.

"Perks of being persuasive." Atlas bristles, clenching his

jaw. "The engagement is off and you know it was nothing more than an arrangement of convenience."

"Yeah." I reply, with bitter sarcasm coating my tongue. "Tell that to her pyromaniac ass."

"P." Cyrus warns, silently reminding me to stay level headed.

"I know." I say, exhaling an exasperated sigh. "I'm done."

He's right. We're here for Alex, and letting Melanie get under my skin won't bring me any closer to finding her.

"She isn't ready." Tristan huffs, talking about me as if I can't hear him. "We'll s... stay in the car. You two go in."

"No." I snap, glaring up at him. "I've got this, alright? It slipped out, but I won't let it happen again. We all need to be there for this plan to work."

The three of them don't seem convinced, but when they say nothing else, I decide to keep quiet for the rest of the drive up the road. This plan will work, but if I slip again, there's no way in hell they're letting me be a part of it.

The architecture of Melanie's home has the same Spanish influence as Maria's Cantina, with a red tile roof, cream stucco walls, crisp archways, and bright pink and green bougainvillea plants climbing up the sides of the building.

The beauty of her home is a stark contrast to the devastation we saw only a few hours ago. The devastation she may very well be responsible for. Alex was the target, but if she was just going to take her, why kill so many innocent people in the process? Why be so fucking reckless?

Atlas pulls up to the main courtyard and throws the car into park. The four of us step out of the car and begin our walk up the long flight of terra cotta colored steps that lead to the second gate.

"Jesus." I say, looking around at the guards carefully watching us. "She has more security than the four of you do."

"She has a lot more enemies too." Atlas remarks, ushering us up to the door.

Once we reach the last gate, it's showtime. The guys all look at me and I nod my head and activate the call box. Within a few seconds, the blank screen flickers to life and Melanie's face enters the frame.

"Hey." She says, her voice sounding both surprised and suspicious as she eyes the four of us carefully. She isn't wearing any makeup and her hair looks drenched. "What's up?"

My lips form into a tight smile as she stares at me expectantly. I wasn't expecting to be so upset at the sight of her. I want to scream in her face. To run in there, throw her down to the ground, and demand that she give me back my sister. But that isn't part of the plan and if this is going to work, I've got to keep up the charade and the show must go on.

"Could we come in?" I ask, gesturing to the four of us. "I really wanted to come by and thank you. You know, for everything."

Melanie cocks her head slightly as she assesses us through the screen. Her nose wrinkles and the fine lines between her eyebrows crease.

"Why the hell not?" She offers, buzzing us into the gate. "I'm almost finished with my laps. Come meet me by the pool."

Once the gate clears, Atlas wraps his arm around the small of my back and escorts me through the grounds, with his brothers trailing a few feet behind us. It's probably a walk he's done countless times in the years he's known Melanie, but I try not to focus on that.

Once we reach the front door, a tall man in his early 30s opens the door and ushers us to the back of the house. He's dressed casually, which is surprising because everyone else we've encountered has been in full uniform, but he's the least of my worries.

As soon as she spots us walk out onto the back patio, Melanie makes a show of stepping out to greet us. She emerges from the pool in a white one piece that emphasizes her naturally tan skin and shakes her wet honey blonde hair. Tiny beads of water trickle down her toned athletic body as she steps towards us and even with no makeup, she's stunning.

"Thank you, Charles." She offers, grabbing her towel as her eyes linger on him for a few seconds longer.

"No problem, Miss Diaz." He says with an easy smile. "If you need anything else, just call." He walks away and heads back into the house without another word.

Melanie watches him leave, and for a second, I wonder who he is. He wasn't familiar with Atlas like Tim was, so he must be new. But what exactly is his job? Before I get too off-track, I shut those thoughts down. We're here for one thing, and one thing only: Alex.

"Thanks for agreeing to see us. Could we talk?" I ask, nodding my head towards her garden. "Alone?"

"Sure." She says, hesitantly as she finishes towel-drying her hair.

This is all part of the plan the guys came up with. Out of the four of us, I'm the only one who can try to get her alone without raising any suspicions. While I distract her, Tristan is going to hack into her phone and see if he can find anything while the other two distract her guards.

Melanie leads us to the garden and once we're out of earshot she speaks up. "I know I said we should hang out, but honestly a text would've been nice. I definitely didn't mean for you to show up at my house whenever you want."

"I would've texted," I say, trying to keep the conversation going, "but I don't have your number."

"Hand it over." She says, giving me her open palm. My eyes flash to her palm then back to her face, and I stare at her like she's sprouted another head. "Your cell phone." She says, cocking a brow. "If you're going to text me, you'll need my number."

I slip my newly recovered cell phone out of my pocket, unlock it, and hand it over to her. Melanie opens the messages app and quickly shoots herself a text. "There you go." She says, handing it back to me. "Now you have no excuse not to text first."

"Thanks." I say, flashing her a fake smile. "I know I should've reached out first. It's just after everything that happened, I feel like we've bonded…"

The next words in the script I practiced escapes me as Melanie turns her head slightly and my eyes latch onto the three fresh red stripes across her left cheek. Stripes that look an awful lot like violent scratch marks.

I try to take a calming breath, but I can't even get enough air in my lungs. Those marks weren't there before. They're fresh. My sister must have scratched her right before she ordered her fucking men to drag her out of that motel room. I know Alex. She wouldn't go quietly, she would fight with everything she had.

Fuck this. There's no need to continue the charade. I have all the proof I need. The marks on her face are too symmetrical to be from an accident and too thick to be from a pet. They're vicious and angry and will probably leave scars. The world stops moving as dark and putrid rage seeps into me. Filling my mind with nothing but violent anger. I painfully squeeze my fists and the numbness feels like it's seeping from my fingers all the way down into my toes. I can't feel anything, or hear anything else. All I see is red.

I don't say anything as I glare at her. I couldn't form words even if I wanted to. I am so in enraged, so mother fucking angry that all rational thought completely vanishes.

I fist Mel's wet hair in a painful vise and yank her to the ground in one rage-filled motion. Her back cracks against the concrete and her shocked expression quickly turns into realization when she locks eyes with me. She knows I know. The horror is written all over her face, and like an animal, I pounce. My left hand wraps her long blonde hair around my wrist as my right hand curls into a fist. I throw my full body weight into a punch and her head rears back as she cries out. I almost feel bad as I watch the blood ooze from her lip, but I can't stop, even if I wanted to.

A distant voice screams at me, but it's like I have tunnel vision. I want to see more blood. I want to watch it spill all over this expensive pearlescent tile and drip down from the garden into her ostentatious infinity pool. The second she touched my sister, she asked for it. I don't care that I shouldn't be doing this. I don't care that it's stupid and dangerous. She wanted to hurt me and now I'm going to hurt her.

A bullet zips by my shoulder, narrowly missing me by a few inches and I look up and freeze.

"That one was a warning." Charles says, pressing the barrel of a hot .45 to my forehead. "Next time, I won't miss. Get the fuck up, now."

I crawl off of Melanie on shaky knees. It's just me, him, and Melanie and, as he helps her to her feet, I realize just how fucked I am.

"Are you okay?" He clips, checking on Mel, but keeping his eyes firmly locked on me.

She stares at him for a few moments. Her face is a mixture of shock and disbelief. "I'm fine." She says, blinking back the tears welling in her eyes as she looks up at him. "Thank you, Charles."

"What should I do with her?" He asks, glaring down at me.

Melanie's eyes flick to me, and she gives me an empty stare. There's no anger behind her eyes at all, only remorse.

"She's left me no choice." She says, looking down at the ground. "Kill her."

Charles gives Melanie a firm nod, and he raises his gun to my forehead with deathly precision. I close my eyes. It's a cowardly move, but I don't want the barrel of a gun to be the last thing I see before I die.

This was always going to be the outcome. I knew that the second I curled my fist around her hair and threw her to the ground. I'm behind enemy lines, and even if she didn't want me to die today, the disrespect I showed her can't just go unanswered. I attacked her in her own home. That action alone is unforgivable.

I hear the click of a gun cocking and I say a silent prayer as my body trembles uncontrollably. *This is it. I'm so sorry, Al.*

"I commend you on your commitment to the job, Charles." Atlas' voice booms and my eyes fly open. "But if you harm a single hair on her head, I'll have no choice but to blow yours off."

MELANIE HISSES as the bag of ice touches her swollen lip. She's seated on one of her lounge chairs as her bodyguard Charles leans over her and tends to her swollen lip.

"Sorry, Miss Diaz." Charles says, tucking a long strand of honey blonde hair behind her ear. "I know it hurts, but we have to stop the swelling."

She looks up at him, and for a moment her eyes soften. "Thanks, Charles." She says, clearing her throat. "Could you give us some space? I have a few things I need to discuss with my *friends*."

Charles gives the four of us a warning glare before giving her a slight bow and quietly retreating into the house.

The way she emphasized the word 'friends' makes me feel like shit. I stand by the edge of the pool and wrap my hands around myself. Everyone else is surrounding her, but I can't stomach the idea of coming face to face with her.

Once the guys arrived, we were at a standstill. Melanie called for more security and the guys jumped in to explain what happened before things got more out of hand. She cancelled the call for reinforcements, but things between us are still far from friendly.

If I had followed the plan like I was supposed to, I

would've found out that the guys had cleared her of any wrongdoing within minutes of us leaving them behind. According to her cell records, she's been home for the last two nights and hasn't been in contact with anyone outside of her compound for the last few days. She didn't take Alex and I feel like such an idiot for assuming she did.

"Let's go over this again." She says, cutting her eyes at me. "You thought I kidnapped your sister?"

"Yeah." I confess as embarrassment flames my cheeks. "I did. But I realize now how stupid that was."

"You don't say." She mumbles with an eye-roll.

Cyrus takes a seat on the lounge beside hers and studies her for a moment. "Where were you last night?" He asks. "If you don't mind me asking."

Melanie throws him a vicious glare as she readjusts the ice pack. "It's like I already told you." She huffs, closing her eyes as she leans back into her lounge. "I was home last night. You can ask Charles for the video footage to prove it. Your psycho girlfriend made a fucking mistake."

"And the s… scratches on your face?" Tristan asks, squinting his eyes to get a better look at them.

"Happened two days ago." She says, bitterly. "You know, when I was helping you guys save her stupid ass. Remind me again why I did that?"

"Because we would've killed you, if you didn't." Atlas clips before letting out a heavy sigh. "How did it happen?"

"After you guys left, Jessie saw an opportunity to escape, and she ran with it. Luckily, after a minor scuffle, I was able to take her down."

Atlas studies her for a second. "She's telling the truth." He says, turning to look out at the infinity pool.

"Of course I am. I didn't even know crazy pants had a sister until you guys mentioned it two days ago. Aside from having no reason to do it, I wouldn't have had enough time to find her, let alone pull off something that horrific."

She's right. And if I had just come into this with a clear head, I would've seen that. Not only did it not make sense for her to go after Alex, but she had no time to make it happen.

"Then who else would target her sister?" Cyrus asks, looking back and forth between the two of us.

Melanie smirks and slowly opens her eyes before glaring at me. "How do you know your sister was the target?"

My brow furrows in confusion. "What do you mean?"

"Isn't it obvious?" She scoffs, flipping her hair back as she sits up in her seat. "I mean, I don't blame you for being dense. It seems to be part of your charm. But you guys have been in this game for years. How do you not see it? A motel room gets trashed. Who's the target?"

"The occupant." The twins retort in unison.

"What's your point, Mel?" Atlas asks, brushing off her not-so-subtle dig at my intelligence.

"One, maybe two people had a big enough issue with Stevie to make something like this happen. One is rotting in prison, courtesy of moi. You're welcome, by the way. And the other is sitting in front of you with a rock solid alibi. What does that tell you?"

"It's someone else." Atlas says, rubbing his chin. "We know that, but there isn't anyone else who knows about her sister."

"My point exactly." She says, with a smug smirk. Seeing the confusion on all of our faces, Melanie shakes her head and sits up in her chair before elaborating. "What if her sister wasn't the intended target?"

"What do you mean?" Tris asks, cocking his head at her. "This was s... some kind of mistake?"

"You said it yourself." She retorts, shrugging her shoulders. "Stevie's enemies are all accounted for, but what about yours?"

"That's impossible." Cyrus says dismissively. "Even if it is one of our enemies, how the hell would they know who her sister is?"

"Therein lies her mistake." Melanie says, leveling her eyes on me. "Tell me, Stevie... who's the room registered to?"

My jaw slacks, and my pulse skyrockets. I don't want to believe it, but everything she's saying makes sense. I caused this. I'm the reason my sister was taken. I spent so much time blaming everyone else, but it was me all along. I'm the monster. Inadvertently or not, I led The Reapers' enemies to my sister. Whatever happens to her from here on out is because of me and the choices I made.

"This attack wasn't someone trying to get back at her, it was someone getting back at the four of you. I'm surprised this didn't click for you sooner, then again, you've never really had anything worth taking. Until now."

The three of them stand there in silence. Their hard faces, completely unreadable. But they know as well as I do that she's right.

"You practically own one of the wealthiest cities in California." Mel adds. "That kind of power comes with a price. And it looks like Stevie's little sister is the one paying for it."

After a few moments of silence, Atlas is the first to speak

up. There's a storm of emotions behind his eyes, but his expression gives nothing away.

"I'm sorry about this, Mel." He says, changing the subject as he rakes a hand through his hair. "We should've never brought you into this."

Melanie scoffs at his apology and turns away.

"I don't need your sympathy." She hisses, laying back down in her chair. "I need you to get the fuck off of my property. This was fun, but the next time you decide to show up at my house again, uninvited, I'll kill you myself."

FOURTEEN

Sweat trickles down my brow as my feet pound against the treadmill. *'Jokes on You' by Charlotte Lawrence* starts up again and the lyrics rip into me. I've been running for almost an hour and my legs already feel like jelly, but I can't stop. If I stop, I'll think. And if I think, I'll feel. Feeling isn't an option right now.

It's been 48 hours since the fire at Dina's, and I'm no closer to finding any answers. Aside from the cryptic message, there's been no contact from Alex's kidnappers. Not even a single fucking demand. Atlas has a meeting set with the best missionaries in the state tomorrow night and I'm hoping something comes from that, but I can't help but feel like we're running around in circles.

I haven't slept much and if the dark circles under my eyes don't immediately give it away, my disheveled appearance does. But I can't bring myself to give a fuck about what I look like when I'm being haunted by my mistakes.

My nightmares are back. Only now, Alex is the one with her face in the dirt screaming for help and I'm standing there watching, helpless to do anything about it.

It felt different when I thought Melanie took her. I knew she wouldn't dare hurt her, because if she did, she'd lose all of her leverage. But now that we know whoever stole her is one of The Reaper's enemies, all bets are off. Who knows what kind of awful torture she'll have to endure at their hands.

The only way to keep my mind off of the horrors she may be going through is to distract myself, and lately, running is the only distraction I can handle. When I run, there's nothing on my mind but the music flowing into my ears and the feel of the ground beneath my feet. It's the only solace from my thoughts, and with how dark my thoughts have been lately, I'd run forever if I could.

As my feet pound against the treadmill, I spot someone else entering the gym from the corner of my eye. *Cyrus.* He tries to make eye contact with me, but the second our eyes meet, I look away. I have nothing to say to him.

Never one to take no for an answer, Cyrus heads straight for my treadmill and stands directly in front of me. I try not to look at him, but his captivating presence is almost impossible to ignore. Even when he's trying to lie low, people notice him.

I look up into his emerald eyes and his face hardens into a scowl. His lips move as he says something to me, but with my music turned up, it's hard to make out the words.

Everything in me wants to ignore him, to pretend that he isn't even here, but he could have news about Alex and that alone is why I give in. At least, that's what I tell myself.

Releasing a sigh, I reluctantly yank the emergency stop on the treadmill, pull out an earbud, and glare at him. "Did you say something?"

Amusement lights his eyes and he flashes me a devious grin. "Just wanted to see how long you were going to be on that."

I deflate. "Are you serious?" I ask, gesturing to the rest of the gym. "There's at least six other treadmills open."

"Fair point," he retorts, nodding his head, "but this one's my favorite."

I give Cyrus an unamused glare. "Really." I deadpan, rolling my eyes. "This specific one?"

"Afraid so." He shrugs, knocking his knuckles against the handle. "So, how much longer?"

Until I can't feel anything anymore. Until the ache in my chest stops hurting so much. "I don't know." I say, squinting at him. "Hours. Use a different one."

"It's fine." He says, shrugging his shoulders with a crooked smile. "I'll wait."

I move to put my earbud back in, but pause when I see he's still staring at me. Under his unwavering gaze, I feel exposed. Like somehow he's seeing beyond the surface and staring straight into my soul. Peering at all the ugly parts of myself I try to keep hidden. He looks like he wants to say something. Like the words are on the tip of his tongue.

"Is there something else?" I ask, cocking a brow at him.

"You should really get some sleep." He says, as his brow furrows. "You look like shit."

Anger flushes my cheeks, but quickly dissipates when I see his eyebrows raise with amusement. He's trying to get a rise out of me, to shake me out of the numbness that's been my security blanket since Alex's kidnapping. I have to hand it to him. It almost worked. *Asshole.*

"Brilliant observation." I say, flashing him a mocking smile as I reattach the emergency stop cord.

He's trying to get under my skin, but I won't let him. Instead of giving in to his little game, I pop my earbud back in, close my eyes, and let myself fall back into the rhythm as the acceleration slowly builds up again. The music flows in and my brain pushes out all thoughts of Cyrus, of Alex, and of all the pain I refuse to feel.

Just when I've hit a steady stride, the treadmill surges to an abrupt stop. My eyes flash open and I look around the room, bewildered. *What the hell?* I glance down at the machine and find the emergency stop cord swinging. I look up and see Cyrus standing there watching my reaction with a smug smirk on his face.

"What is it this time?" I spit, all hints of playfulness gone from my tone.

"Why are you down here so late?" He asks, cocking his head as his emerald eyes stare into the depths of my consciousness. "Having trouble sleeping?"

"I came down here to run." I say, narrowing my eyes at him. "The sooner you let me get to it, the sooner you'll have the machine all to yourself."

Cyrus frowns as he crosses his sleeved arms across his chest. "Fine. Stick with what you know."

I scoff and glare back at him. "What the hell is that supposed to mean?" I ask.

"Forget it, Princess." He says, stepping away from me. "There are some things you'll never be ready to hear."

I hop off of the treadmill and follow his retreat. "No, you felt the need to say it." I say, getting into his face. "Elaborate."

Cyrus deliberates for a moment before answering me. "You're a runner." He says, throwing his hands up. "Let's be honest, it's what you do best, and it's what you're doing right now. You may be here, but in that fucking head of yours, you are miles away."

I shake my head in denial. "That's not true."

Cyrus presses closer. "Then why is it that this is the first time you've so much as looked me in the eye since the fire?" He asks, searching my eyes.

"Because I have nothing to say." I mumble, avoiding his penetrating gaze.

"Why is that?" He asks, cocking his head.

Instead of dignifying him with a response, I shut my mouth, slip in my earbuds again, and storm back to my treadmill. I don't want to talk about this. I don't want to talk about anything.

Just as I pick up my pace again, Cyrus rips the emergency stop cord right in front of my face and levels an angry glare at me. I say nothing as I grab the cord and grip it in my hands. *This little game of his is fucking ridiculous and I want no part in it.*

"The Silence" by The Veronicas plays in my head and I close my eyes and turn the volume up higher. I'm done

playing into his antics. I reattach the emergency stop and pick up my pace again.

After a few seconds, I break into a sprint, and without warning, the machine sputters to stop. I let out an angry sigh and reach for the cord with my eyes still firmly shut. I expect to find it unattached again, but when I feel for it, I find the cord just as I left it.

I flick my eyes open and come face-to-face with Cyrus holding what appears to be the power cord. He levels a vicious glare at me as he tosses the cord to the ground before taking out one of my earbuds. "We're talking whether you want to or not."

"Actually," I say, hopping off of the treadmill and snatching my earbud back, "we're not. I was finished, anyway."

I don't want to cut my run short, but anything is better than being forced to face him and all the questions behind his eyes.

I storm towards the exit and can feel Cyrus following me right on my heels. "Fuck, Stevie!" He yells, chasing after me. "Fight me. Scream at me. Show me something, Princess. I'd rather feel your hate than feel nothing at all."

I twist around to face him. "I don't hate you." I sneer, cutting my eyes at him. "Not everything is about you, Cyrus."

"Bullshit." He challenges, maneuvering around me to block the exit. "I see it all over your face. You'd love nothing more than to punch me in my face right now. Admit it."

"Fine, I hate you." I deadpan. "Now move the fuck out of the way."

He shakes his head with a smile. "Finally, a step in the right direction, but you're still angry. I see it. Take a shot." He says, patting the side of his face for emphasis. "One solid punch to get all the hate out of your system."

I look up at him incredulously. "I'm not going to punch you."

"Why?" He asks, cocking a brow. "Scared you might like it?"

"No. Unlike you, I don't resort to violence to solve all my problems."

"I can think of a few instances where that's exactly what you've done. Hit me, P. You know you want to."

I shake my head in denial. "No."

"Do it." He says, getting closer to my face. "Come on. Show me what you got."

Maybe it's his incessant pestering. Maybe it's the fact that he interrupted the one activity I used to escape from my thoughts. Maybe it's just his own bad fucking timing. Any other day, I would've never taken him up on the offer. But as I stare at the stupid smirk on his face and think about all the bullshit that I've been through since I met him and his brothers, I stop overthinking for once in my life and I act.

Forming a fist with my right hand, I wind back slightly and throw everything I have in a solid punch to his jaw. My body snaps forward and as my fist zeroes in on his jaw, Cyrus realizes what's happening and ducks out of the way inches before my fist collides with his face.

"Holy shit!" He exclaims, raising his brows. "You were actually going to hit me." His face contorts in mock shock as he presses his hand to his heart. "I'm hurt, Princess. Arguing is one thing, but resorting to violence? This is a cry for help."

"You are such an asshole." I clip, shoving him back.

Instead of recovering, like we both know he easily

could've, he wraps his hands around my waist at the last minute and lets the force of my shove pull us both down to the mat.

I land on top of Cyrus and our foreheads knock together on impact. I pull back, scowling down at him as I rub the sting away. "God, Cyrus." I growl, wiggling to try to untangle myself from his hold. "What the fuck is your prob—"

My eyes widen and I lose all train of thought as I feel *something* harden underneath me.

Seeing my obvious reaction, Cyrus flashes me a grin. "What's the matter, Princess?" He gloats, releasing his hold to wrap his arms behind his head. "Big cock got your tongue?"

For a moment, I'm drunk on the thought of all the dirty things he could do to me in this room, but the smug grin on his face sobers me up. *No.* He caught me off guard, but I won't let it happen again.

I glare down at him and put on my best bored expression. "Hardly." I huff, ignoring the impressive bulge pressing against me. "It isn't anything that exciting."

His cocky grin fades and the expression behind his eyes transforms. Instead of my insult pushing him away, like I expected it to, I see the unmistakable gleam of challenge in his eyes.

Without saying another word, his hands latch onto my hips and he grinds my body up and down his hard bulge once. The layers of fabric between us should dull the sensation, but it's almost as if the barriers between us heighten it. My pussy painfully throbs, yearning for the temptation he's dangling in front of us.

Cyrus releases my hips and studies my expression.

"Everything okay, P?" He asks, feigning innocence as he tries to hold back his smile. "You look a little... unsettled."

"I'm fine." I bite back, planting my feet on the ground to stand up. Cyrus latches onto my hips and grinds my body against his cock again, and my mind turns into jelly. *Fuck.* I think, shaking my head. *How can someone so infuriating feel this good?*

"You want me." Cyrus notes, as he deliciously glides my covered pussy up and down the length of his cock. "You're just too fucking angry to admit it."

He's right. I am angry. At him. At myself. At the world. But feeling his cock harden underneath me is the best kind of distraction and honestly, my anger is the last thing on my mind.

"Admit it, Princess." He taunts, sliding my hips against him at a painfully slow pace. "You want this. All you have to do is say the word..." He trails off, jutting his hips forward for emphasis. "And this cock is yours."

Cyrus slides my center down his covered cock so slowly that for a second it feels like time has stopped. My pussy throbs and the pain is borderline excruciating. All I can think about is more. More movement, more sensation, more of him. "Cy, please." I plead, looking up into his eyes. "I need this."

Even though he coaxed it out of me, I mean what I'm saying; I need this. In more ways than he could imagine. I've been so disconnected from everyone. So consumed with my anger that I'm starting to feel like I'm losing myself. I need him to help me release some of this anger before it swallows me whole.

"Fuck." He groans, pulling me in for a sensual kiss before yanking off his t-shirt. "I thought you'd never ask."

I kiss him back and allow our tongues to swirl against each other before pinning his lower lip between my teeth. "You're such a dick." I say, releasing his lip as I gather the edge of my hoodie in my hands and toss it over my head.

"I am." He admits, with a nod of his head. "But a sick part of you loves it."

I pull him in again for another kiss and can't help but grin. He's right. He infuriates me. But a part of me, the dickmatized, masochistic, crazy part, loves everything about it. Cyrus has this innate magnetism that pulls people in, and even when I try to fight it, I know there's no real point. I could try to escape, but I'll always find a way back into his pull.

I stare into his emerald eyes as my fingers run along the hard ridges of his bare, tattooed stomach. The heat in his stare is enough to start a fire, but that isn't what makes me turn away. Beyond the fire and beyond the lust, I see a look in Cy's eyes I've never seen before. Something deeper. More sacred. Something that feels a lot like love.

Instead of dwelling on what this could mean for us, I close my eyes and allow myself to fall back into the moment. Whatever this is, or whatever this means, doesn't matter. All that matters is what we want and the friction building between our bodies.

Cyrus grinds my body against his harder and even though we're still partially clothed, it feels innately dirty. Like we're doing something we shouldn't. I plant my hands against his chest and grind against him harder, letting out a little moan every time his cock rubs against my sensitive clit in just the right way.

Cyrus slaps my ass with a crack of his wrist and smirks.

"These," He remarks, rubbing away the sting. "Fucking sexy."

He wraps his hands around my ass and grips the stretchy black fabric of my shorts tightly. With no effort at all, he rips it down the seam, leaving a massive hole in the center. He does the same with my thong, nearly ripping it off of my body completely. Cold air hits my sensitive pussy and my whole body shivers.

"Don't worry, Princess." Cyrus says, reaching between us to slap my bare pussy. "I'll buy you new ones."

Cyrus licks the tips of his fingers, reaches between us and starts brushing his fingers against my sensitive clit. My eyes roll into the back of my head as heat starts to build inside of me. His touch feels so good, and my whole body twitches with each tantalizing brush of his fingers. I'm hot, so fucking hot, and all I want to do is shed the fabric still sandwiched between us.

Rising to my knees, I kick off my sneakers, reach for my sports bra and pull it up over my head. The shorts can stay, but I need to shed everything else. I want to feel as close to him as possible. Following my lead, Cyrus sheds the rest of his clothing as he stares at me hungrily.

We lock eyes with each other, and for a moment, we just take each other in. It feels monumental. Like there's no going back after this. If I give myself to him now, I'm not only accepting who he is, but everything he's done in the past. The games. The cruel words. Everything. But I don't want to think anymore. Not when it comes to my feelings for Cyrus Cole.

I climb back on his lap, and hold my breath as Cy guides himself towards my entrance. He inches the tip in and I let out a little sigh as I adjust to the stretch. I study his face as my pussy takes him in. His pupils dilate and his brow furrows in concentration as I slowly slide myself up and down his shaft.

"Yes, Princess." He coaxes, digging his fingers into the flesh of my hips. "Fuck yourself just like that."

I move faster, feeling empowered by his filthy words. I bounce on him over and over again until I see the moment Cy becomes maddened with lust.

Cy sits up and sinks his teeth into the side of my neck as he takes over the strokes. Fucking me hard as the sting from his bite sends chills down my spine. Everything about the way he fucks me feels possessive, and it hurts in the best way possible.

He's insatiable, and as my tits bounce in his face, his greedy mouth latches onto one of my nipples and bites down, hard. His hands find my ass cheeks and he spreads them so wide as he pounds into me, it feels like his cock is splitting me in half.

I'm thrown into a state of catatonic bliss as the pain and pleasure he gives me compete for my undivided attention. His teeth clamp down on my nipple and I throw my head back and moan. "Oh, my god. That feels so fucking good."

As his thick cock pulls a mind-blowing orgasm out of me, I pound my fist against his chest and curse his name. "Cyrus. Cyrus. Oh my fucking god, Cy—"

Cyrus silences my curse with a filthy kiss as his hips move more furiously. The stimulus is too much and I'm on the precipice of pushing him when I feel his muscles stiffen and he releases a powerful orgasm of his own as tongue dances with mine.

The two of us sit there for a moment with bodies intertwined, neither of us willing to be the first to part. After a few minutes, I'm the first to move, and Cyrus presses his forehead against mine.

"Not that exciting, huh?" He teases, wrapping his arms around me and squeezing me tightly.

"Don't get it twisted, Cole." I say, fighting the smile threatening to form on my lips. "I still hate you."

Cyrus groans as I pull myself off of him and fall to the ground. I roll out on my back and lay there for a second just trying to catch my breath.

"You can hate me. For now." He smirks, folding his arms behind his head. "But one day, P. You're going to love me."

"You're ridiculous." I say, shaking my head as I lean against my elbows. "For the record, Cy. I don't hate you." I say, looking up at the dark beams running along the ceiling.

"Come on, there's a little hate in there. I feel it."

"I hate myself." I confess. "Maybe that's what you're feeling?"

"Princess, don't blame—"

"Don't." I say, sitting up and pulling my knees to my chest. "Don't try to make me feel better." I release a breath and wrap my arms around my knees before continuing. "What happened to Alex isn't anyone's fault, but my own. I knew the risks of being with you guys and I went along with it, anyway. Alex is gone because of my choices. Not yours. I'm an awful person and I don't deserve anyone's love."

I blink back the tears threatening to fall from my eyes. I will not sit here and feel sorry for myself. I've got myself into this mess and I have to deal with the fucking consequences and figure my own way out.

"That's not true." He says, shifting to a seated position to run his hands along my bare arms.

"Yes, it is." I say, glaring back at him. "You just don't see."

"I know what the fuck I see, P." He says, pulling me back into his lap. "I see someone who's kind. And strong. Someone who would do whatever it takes to protect the people she loves. Tell me, does that sound like someone who doesn't deserve love?"

I lean back in his powerful arms and absorb the attention I know I don't deserve. Despite what he says, I know I'll never be able to right my wrongs. To undo whatever damage is being done to my sister, but if Cyrus can still look at me and see someone who deserves to be loved. Maybe after we save her, and everything is said and done, I'll be able to look at myself in the same light. Maybe.

FIFTEEN

Chewing on my thumbnail, I shoot a scathing glance at the receptionist as she shoves another piece of bright red cherry bubblegum into her mouth. It's her third piece in the last thirty minutes, so either the gum she buys is shit or I'm stuck in some type of psychological torture device. She pops her gum and I flinch, narrowing my eyes at her as I grit my teeth. *People who pop their gum deserve jail time.*

She notices my reaction and offers me a timid smile. "Sorry." She says with a tiny wince. "Still getting used to the echo in here."

She's new. It makes sense. Though it doesn't make her grate against my nerves any less.

Why the hell am I even here?

When Atlas told me we were meeting with a team of lethal mercenaries, I expected to meet them in some gritty underground parking garage, or at some shady looking abandoned restaurant. No way could I have ever imagined we'd meet them in some fancy high rise in the middle of the business district.

"You sure I can't get you a cup of coffee or something?" The receptionist asks again for what feels like the hundredth time.

I get why she's being so attentive. From what I can tell, Creed Enterprises owns the entire floor, and apart from the two of us, no one has entered or left this ostentatious lobby in the last forty minutes.

"I'm fine." I bite out, a little harsher than I intend to.

It isn't her fault I'm on edge. Atlas is the one who abandoned me out here.

As soon as we arrived, Creed and his men came out, gave me a dismissive glance, steered Atlas towards the conference room, and firmly shut the door behind them. I expected Atlas to realize the mistake and circle back for me, but when that didn't happen, I realized it must've been part of his plan all along.

From the very beginning, Atlas was hesitant to let me come with him. I wanted to hear what these specially trained men plan to do to find my sister, but he kept insisting that it would be better if he spoke with them alone. The only reason

I could come today was because I convinced the twins to leave me behind. With Ezra missing in action and no one else at home to monitor me, Atlas had no choice but to let me come.

But it ended up being all for nothing. He's in there, negotiating terms with some of the most lethal mercenaries in the country, while I'm in the lobby alone looking completely overdressed in a red silk minidress that barely covers my ass.

I drum my fingertips against my bare knees and glare up at the clock on the wall. *God.* Time is moving so damn slowly. *What's taking them so long in there?*

I pull out my cell phone and stare at the blank screen. A normal person would call their friends to pass the time, but the only real friend I have is Alex, and her phone is out of commission.

I mindlessly pull up my text messages anyway, needing something to help pass the time. As soon as I do, a text from an unknown number shows up in my inbox. *Weird timing.* I open the message to get a better look and wait for the grey box to display on the screen.

Unknown Number: The Reapers won't help you find her, but I will.

My whole body freezes as I stare down at my phone in disbelief. An eerie feeling sinks in, and I look up from the screen and scan my surroundings. It feels like I'm being watched, but there's still no one else in the room besides me and the receptionist. *Who the hell is this?*

Who are you?

I type out, but before hitting send, I change my mind and quickly delete the question. I shouldn't respond to them. At the very least, not until I show Atlas.

Three grey dots pop up in the text conversation and my heart skips a beat.

The eerie feeling creeps up again and I look up from my phone and glance around the room again just to make sure I'm still alone. Could this person know something we don't?

Unknown Number: The Reapers will always serve The Reapers. If you don't believe me, ask yourself, would saving her benefit them? If the answer is no, then they aren't on your side.

Jesus.

I stare at the screen, gnawing on my lower lip, as I think about what to say back to them. There's no doubt whoever this is knows The Reapers intimately. But what they're saying is fucking crazy. I know The Reapers and everything they've done so far has been to help me. They want my sister back just as much as I do. *Don't they?*

"Everything okay?"

The sound of Atlas's smooth, velvety voice sends my heart leaping into my stomach.

"Y- Yeah." I stammer, deleting the message chain before he can see it. "I was just playing some silly game on my phone and got distracted."

Atlas offers me a small smile before gesturing for me to follow him out. I don't like hiding things from him, but something about what the text said struck a nerve.

The more that I think about it, the more that I realize that whoever sent the message isn't wrong. The Reapers have always put their own needs above everyone else's. Lately, I've become one of those needs, but that doesn't give me any guarantees for Alex.

"How did it go?" I ask, standing up from my chair and moving to walk beside him.

Instead of answering right away, Atlas leads us to the sleek metal elevator and waits for the doors to close before continuing.

"According to their sources," He says, sinking his hands into the pockets of his light grey suit pants, "in the days leading up to the fire, there were a few different men at Hell's Tavern asking questions about you."

I grimace. The thought of my name being on any stranger's lips unnerves me. "That's weird; but are we sure it's a lead?"

The last appearance I made at Hell's Tavern didn't exactly go smoothly, and I'm sure I made a lasting impression on a few of the guests who witnessed the fight between Melanie and me up close and personal.

Atlas locks his eyes on me before answering. "They didn't just want to know about you, they wanted to know about your importance to us."

"Any idea who they were?"

Atlas hesitates. Not long enough for someone not paying attention to take notice, but long enough for me to question why.

"No. No names. Whoever it was, wasn't from here, and it'd be nearly impossible to search the cameras. We have unfamiliar faces coming in and out of the club every night."

"So we're back to square one." I say, knocking the back of my head against the elevator wall.

"Not exactly." He says, watching the floor numbers change as we make our descent. "The Mercenaries will take over the search for Alex from here on out. If anyone can find her, it'll be them."

"Good." I say, with a firm nod. "With all of us searching, we'll figure out who has her."

"No." Atlas says, pinning me with a hard glare. "One of their only stipulations for taking the job is that we aren't allowed to tamper with their investigation. We can't go rogue. And any information we receive goes straight to them."

"But wouldn't it make more sense to have as many hands on deck as possible?" I ask.

"This is what they do. They find people that don't want to be found. My brothers and I have our own ways of getting information, but with something like this, we need to leave it up to the experts."

The surrounding air drops a couple of degrees and I cross my arms over my chest.

"So you're giving up." I say, pressing my lips into a tight line. *Maybe whoever texted me was right. Maybe The Reapers won't help me.*

"We aren't giving up anything. Nothing is changing. Our men will still keep an eye out, but we need to let The Mercenaries do their job. We're leaving the search to them. Is that clear?"

"Crystal." I bite back with my eyes fixed on the elevator doors as they glide open. Without waiting for him, I step out and head straight for the parking garage.

I make my way back to Atlas' white Porsche in silence. I can hear him trailing a few steps behind me, but I don't slow down. He says they aren't giving up, that he and his men have done everything they can, but why can't I shake the feeling I'm being lied to?

"Why did you let me come with you?" I snap, my frustration with him boiling over as I turn around to face him. "What, was I just there to be arm candy and make you look good?"

Atlas stops moving and levels his golden brown eyes on me.

"No." He fumes with narrowed eyes. "The Mercenaries are a highly sought after team of trained assassins. It was almost impossible to book that meeting with them. It took a lot of favors and a lot of negotiations to make it happen. I planned to go back for you, but they insisted we keep the negotiations between us. It had nothing to do with you."

I stand there for a moment and stare at him.

"I'm sorry." I say, and this time, I actually mean it. I'm not sure why, but it's almost like I want to see the bad in him. The bad and all of them, really. But they keep exceeding my expectations. Just when I think they're going to zig, they fucking zag and throw me into a tailspin.

"It's fine. I knew this would be a lot for you to deal with so soon after your sister's—" He cuts off the rest of his sentence when he notices my glare, but I already received his message loud and clear.

"Here." He says tossing me a set of keys he plucked out of his pocket.

"What's this for?" I ask, dangling the keys between my index finger and thumb.

"I have somewhere else I need to be." He says, pulling out his cellphone. "And I'm sure by now you know the way home."

I do, but I still don't understand why.

"You're letting me drive myself home?" I ask, narrowing my eyes at him. "Why?"

"What you said the other night didn't sit right with me. This is my way of showing you things have changed."

My eyebrows knit together in a scowl.

"You're letting me go." I say, cocking a brow at him. "Without an escort?"

"I trust you." He says, evenly. "Now go. My driver should be here in a few minutes."

I look down at the set of keys in my hand and grip them tightly as my emotions threaten to surface. *He really does trust me.*

"Where are you going?" I ask, trying my best to hide the emotion in my voice.

"Hell's Tavern. I'm due for an appearance. While I'm there, I'll see if I can catch wind of anything."

I smirk up at him. "I thought there were stipulations."

"There are, but if The Mercenaries tried to scope out Hell's Tavern, people would immediately know something was up. Besides, no one knows the ins and outs of my club better than I do."

"I'm coming with you." I say, keeping my head held high. "If your theories are correct, whoever took Alex meant to take me. Maybe seeing me alive will make them realize their mistake and they'll come after me instead. At the very least I'll be able to notice if something feels off with someone."

Atlas assesses me, as if he's trying to decide what to do next. I'm tired of sitting on the sidelines and waiting for something to happen. I need this. Not just for Alex's sake, but for my own too.

A frown forms on his face before he responds. "I'm not going to willingly put you in danger."

"Please." I beg softly, looking up at him with pleading eyes. "If I go back home, I'll be alone, and if I'm alone too long, I'll think about her. Doing this gives me purpose."

Atlas takes a step closer and pulls me into his chest. "Stevie, we're going to find her." He says, leaning back to look me in the eye. "Whoever has her, whatever plan they have, they need her alive."

"I know." I say, blinking back the tears threatening to well in my eyes. "But there's a lot of damage you can cause to a person before you kill them. That's the part I'm worried about."

For a moment, we stand in the middle of the parking garage, just wrapped in each other's embrace. Atlas grips me so tightly it's borderline painful. Like I'm slipping through his fingers, but if he holds on tightly enough, I'll never leave his side. And I hold him like he's the home I never had but always wanted. Like he's the shelter from the storm that's been my life. We stand like that for a few minutes, just savoring the moment and feeling the history between us come full circle.

When our hug finally breaks, Atlas is the first to speak. "I hate to admit it," he says, "but your plan may be the best option we have. In order for it to work, we need to make sure every single eye is on you the second you walk into that building."

"How do we do that?" I ask.

"I've got an idea." He smirks as his eyes slowly drink me in. "Get in the driver's seat. You're well overdue for a grand entrance."

SIXTEEN

Thirty minutes later and the two of us pull up to the entrance of Hell's Tavern. We haven't even gotten out of the car yet, but I can already feel the vibration of the EDM music pumping through the speakers. I look at the long line of people waiting outside and bristle. Anyone of them could've played a part in Alex's disappearance.

"Are you sure you want to do this?" Atlas asks, linking his fingers with mine.

I look down at our intertwined hands, and the tender

moment is bittersweet. I never thought we'd get here. Allowing ourselves to express our emotions for each other so freely, like this. And now it's like at any moment the closeness I feel with him could be stripped away. I don't want to lose him, but I know if something happens to my sister, things with us will never be the same.

"It's the only thing I can do." I respond, squeezing his hand a little tighter. "It keeps me busy, which is a good thing. You know how I am with idle hands."

Atlas gives me a smirk before stepping out of the car to meet me on the driver's side. He helps me out and gently glides his arm over my shoulder in a casual sign of possession that sends a little thrill up my spine. The crowd's eyes follow our every move, but Atlas seems utterly unfazed. His stride is powerful and his head held high as he ushers me straight up to the front door.

"They're all staring at us." I whisper as I tuck in closer to his side.

"Not us, Kitten." He says as his lips form into a devilish grin. "You."

His statement gives me pause, and for a second my feet stop moving. "Why are they staring at me?" I hiss, looking up into his eyes.

"It's not every day a queen arrives to claim her throne."

A new wave of nervousness hits me. *That's it, isn't it?* This visit isn't just about finding Alex. It's about sending a message. The last time I was here, I was a toy, brought in solely for The Reapers' amusement, but that isn't my role in their lives anymore.

Tonight, as I walk into the building under Atlas's muscular arm, I'm staking a claim on something I never knew existed.

I'm letting his entire world know I'm the one he chose. I'm his queen. I have no doubt in my mind that my new title will be tested, but I've never been more ready to fight for what's mine.

Heavy is the crown.

"IF YOU NEED anything else at all, just ask."

The red-headed server shoots Atlas a flirtatious wink and I jerk my cocktail up from the table and slurp it loudly. Her throaty baby voice is obnoxious, and if I'm going to have to sit through this bullshit any longer, I'll need much more alcohol.

It wouldn't be so bad if it were just her, but there seems to be an ever rotating merry-go-round of slutty servers in this place and she's just one of the many we've seen tonight.

Initially, I wrote off their blatant flirting as part of the normal service the girls here offer, but five different women have visited our lounge at least ten times within the hour. And during every single visit, they only focus their eyes on Atlas.

"I'll take another." I say abruptly, shaking my empty glass for emphasis. I've been sucking on melted ice for the last thirty minutes, not that any of them have noticed.

She shoots me an annoyed glare and rips my glass out of my hand.

"I'll have that right out for you." She hisses, all sweetness from her voice suddenly gone.

"Awesome." I say, flashing her a mocking smile.

She could stand to be knocked down a few pegs, and if she keeps talking to me like that, I'll be happy to be the one to do it.

Atlas levels his eyes on me and cocks his brow with an amused look in his eyes.

"What?" I ask, flipping my hair off of my bare shoulder.

"Nothing." He says, fighting a smile.

"I needed a drink."

"Uh, huh." He says, leaning into me. "You know, if I didn't know you any better, I'd say you were jealous."

I turn away from him and smooth down my dress. "I'm not jealous. I just have a hard time respecting people that don't understand boundaries. They're working right now, but all they seem to care about is flirting their boney asses off. Other patrons of the club are suffering because of their neglect. Excuse me for caring about your business."

"If you say so, Kitten." Atlas says, letting out a light-hearted laugh before taking another sip of his drink. "Still, I probably wouldn't trust any drink she brings you after that interaction."

My smile falls.

Damnit.

"Ugh." I say, rolling my eyes as I stand up from my seat. "You're right. I'm going to head to the bar. Do you want anything?"

Atlas gestures to the four other Jack & Cokes, still waiting for him on the coffee table. The sight only fuels my annoyance, and I grit my teeth with a sneer. Of course, they made it a point to refill his fucking drink every visit. *Stupid asshole servers.*

"Calm down, Kitten." He says, shaking his head with a smile. "She's testing you. They all are."

"Did I mention I've always been terrible at tests?"

Atlas only shakes his head in response as he takes another slow sip of his whisky. As I walk past him, I gently pat him on his shoulder and make my way towards the bar. The whole point of coming here was to get some intel on Alex's kidnappers and try to find out who the hell has been asking about me. But the only thing we've done is summon an army of skanks. It's like, with Jessie no longer around to keep them in line, the girls have gone wild.

I approach the bar and lean against the cool granite countertop as I wait for service and silently thank my lucky stars that none of the bartenders hate me. Yet. One of the male bartenders approaches me and I quickly put in a drink order for two hellhounds and take a seat while I wait. From the peripheral of my vision, I see a large body sink into the seat next to me and turn to face me.

"We meet again." It only takes me a second to recognize who it is. But once I do, it's a voice I'd recognize anywhere. Dimitri.

"Go away, Dimitri."

"Now, now. That's no way to talk to a friend. Besides, I come bearing peace."

I pivot slightly in his direction and slowly level my eyes at him. "Somehow I find that incredibly hard to believe."

He nods his head as he swirls his glass of rich brown liquid. "That's understandable." He says, looking up at me with the deepest blue eyes I've ever seen. I don't remember them being this captivating. Then again, I try my hardest not to remember anything about that night.

"We didn't have the best first impressions of each other." He says. "But I hope you now see my intention was never to hurt you. They led me to believe you were nothing to them. Merely a toy. And I'm embarrassed to say I acted accordingly. I apologize for my behavior, Kroshka. Truly. But I assure you, in a world full of enemies, I am one of the few you can trust."

"Do us both a favor?" I ask, grateful to see the bartender placing the garnishes on my drinks. "Save the excuses for someone who gives a shit."

I thank the bartender, slide a twenty onto the bar top, and gather the two glasses in my hands. Dimitri can try to twist the narrative all he wants, but he knows what he did was wrong. My grievance with him may be on the back burner right now, but that doesn't mean I'm letting him get away with it. Not by a long shot.

I take a step away from the bar and turn on my heel to make my way back to Atlas.

"You never responded to my text." He calls out.

I freeze in place as my thoughts race. *That couldn't have been him, could it?* I glanced at my phone the entire drive here, debating on whether to text the number back. I was planning on telling Atlas and having his guys see if they can trace the number. But a small part of me, the ugly distrusting part, thought it was better to keep it to myself. I still hadn't decided what to do with it yet, but now it looks like I won't have to.

"What text?" I ask, feigning ignorance. I'm not stupid enough to take his bait that easily. If it was him, he needs to prove it.

"It's good to be distrusting." He remarks, leaning closer to my back. "You should be wary of everyone, including your men."

I shake my head as my upper lip curls.

"I have known them for a long time." He whispers, his warm breath cascading down my bare shoulders. "Long before you ever knew who they were. One fact about them has always remained true: The Cole brothers look out for The Cole brothers. No one else."

"And what about you?" I ask, turning around to face him. "What makes you different? Why the hell would you want to help me?" I have no idea why I'm even entertaining this conversation, but something inside of me wants to hear what he has to say.

"You're right." He says, shrugging his muscular shoulders as he leans back against the bar. "I have no real cause. No vested interest in any of this. But unlike my brothers, I have a conscience and as much as you may not want to believe it, I regret our first encounter. Helping you find your sister is my way of making up for that."

I mull over his words for a moment and study his features for any signs of a lie. His words feel like they're true, but I can no longer simply trust my gut. Not with so much at stake.

"You want to make it up to me? Fine. But if we're doing this, everything goes through Atlas. I'm not hiding anything from them."

"That is disappointing, Kroshka. Unfortunately for you, I'm not nearly as trusting of them as you seem to be. I have resources I feel will help, but I can't, in good conscience, hand it over to them. They'll only end up betraying you. If you want my help, you'll have to accept it without them."

"No deal." I say, shaking my head. "We'll find her without you. And just so you know, you're wrong about them. They would never do anything to betray me."

"Is that so?" He asks, staring into my eyes so hard it feels like he's peering into my soul. "Then might I suggest not returning to your table just yet. I think you've had enough disappointment to last you a lifetime."

Against Dimitri's suggestion and against my better judgment, I turn around and the sight I see punches me straight in the gut. The servers. The stupid, big-titted tramp whores are hanging all over Atlas. Circling him like a group of hyenas.

I know it's unfair for me to expect fidelity when I'm in a relationship with his brothers, but that doesn't stop the jealousy from pouring into me.

The world stops moving as I barrel my way towards Atlas. I painfully grip the icy drinks in my hands and the numbness feels like it's seeping from my fingers all the way down into my toes.

I stop steps in front of the group and the girls are too distracted by Atlas to notice my presence. Ironically enough, the red-head showed up with my hellhound after all and by the looks of it, she "accidentally" spilled it all over Atlas. Luckily for him, the other servers were right there, ready to help her clean up her silly mistake.

I loudly clear my throat, expecting them to scatter as soon as they see me, but none of them make a move to leave. *Assholes*. Atlas glances up and we lock eyes. There's no hint of embarrassment or shame in his eyes, just mild amusement. I have nothing to worry about and his lack of response proves it. Still, these bitches need to go.

I gesture for him to do something about it, but he says nothing in response. Instead, he looks around the room before glaring back at me as if to say, "the entire crowd is watching. What are you going to do about this?"

He's right. If I let him take the reins on this, I'll end up looking weak and insecure and I'll never get the respect I deserve.

"Excuse me." I say, a little more softly than I intend to. I wait for some kind of reaction, but when I don't get one; I try again. "Excuse me." I repeat, a little stronger this time, and I see the five women surrounding him visibly bristle. "Hey!" I snap. Forgoing my attempt at politeness all together.

The red-headed server jerks her head in my direction and sneers as she looks me up and down. She's sitting beside Atlas and is in the middle of patting down his lap with tiny black cocktail napkins.

"Can we help you?" She sneers, cocking a brow at me.

"You're in my seat." I say calmly, fighting the instinct to sneer back at her. My voice is cool, detached even, and there's no hint of the hostility brewing inside of me.

"Oh, sweetheart." She laughs, stepping up to her full height as she smooths down her royal blue minidress. "I'm sure he had fun with you, but with Melanie out of the picture & Jessie finally gone, the world is his oyster and he has much better options now. I think it's time you leave, before you really embarrass yourself."

I take a step back, and her face radiates with delight. She thinks she's won and, based on the looks on their faces, the other servers think so too. But Atlas knows better. His eyes haven't left mine since I stepped back into the lounge and I can see the thoughts swirling inside of his head. He's wondering what I'll do next. How I'll handle this woman's blatant disrespect.

The old Stevie would've attacked. She would've ripped the red hair out of her head and beat her in the face until she felt better. But I've changed a lot since the first time I visited Hell's Tavern. Violence won't be enough to deter these women, not by a long shot. They want the money and power that comes along with being with a man like Atlas, and will go through hell to get it. *No.* To earn my rightful place in this world, I need to show them that Atlas will never choose anybody else but me. That I am the queen he and his brothers have chosen.

"Ladies." I call out, my voice carrying all the power and exuberance of royalty as I address the room. "It's time to leave. Now."

"We aren't done yet." The red-head sneers, acting as their spokesperson yet again.

I level my eyes on her and offer her a wintry smile. "You seem like a smart girl… um…" I trail off, signaling for her to fill in the blank.

"Katie." She finishes for me, wrapping her arms across her chest as her eyes flick back and forth between me and her pack of hyenas.

"Katie." I repeat back, flashing her a smile. "We haven't been properly introduced yet, so I'm going to give you the benefit of the doubt here. I'm Stevie, and right now, you still being here after I politely asked you to leave is crossing a fucking line."

The red-head narrows her eyes at me. "I know who you are." She spouts, shaking her head indignantly at me. "Jessie told us all about The Reapers' new little toy." She says, giving the other servers a knowing grin.

I let out a little laugh before narrowing my eyes at her. "I'm so glad she's kept you in the know. Did she mention the only reason she's still breathing is because I spared her life?" I ask, cocking my head at her. Katie's smile falters and a shit-eating grin forms on my face. "How about the fact that after we were done with her and her men, there wasn't a single spot on the floor not coated in blood?"

Katie's eyes shift around the room uncomfortably, but she doesn't say a word.

"I didn't think so." I say, shaking my head with a sad smile. "This will be my one and only warning." I call out, wanting everyone within earshot to hear. "The Reapers are mine and if you or anyone else ever disrespects me again, I won't have security escort you out. I'll snap your fucking neck myself, just to prove that I can."

I shoulder past her, and the other servers scatter the second they see me coming.

Katie stares at us with her mouth agape and her eyes rounded. "You-you can't just threaten us like that." Katie huffs, planting her hands on her hips. "We're his employees. Atlas, aren't you going to do something about this?"

"You're right." Atlas says, as his eyes roam the length of my body hungrily. "I definitely need to do something about her."

Without bothering to give Katie another glance, he leans back against the blue suede sofa and locks eyes with me. "Come, Kitten." He orders, patting his muscular thigh with a smirk. "Find out what Daddy thinks about your behavior."

My face breaks into a smile when I hear my pet name slip from his lips. With anyone else, I'd view it as a slip up and move on, but with him, it's different. Atlas is a very calculated man. He knows the crowd is watching and is lingering on every word we say. Calling me "Kitten" in front of them isn't just a cute moment between the two of us, it's a way of staking a claim on me. It's showing everyone a glimpse at the deeper connection we have. If anyone was unsure of my importance in his life, calling me by my pet name just clarified it.

I can't help but smile at the hint of a challenge in his eyes. He's gauging me, seeing if I'll give in to his temptation. Everything about this moment feels so visceral. The way his intoxicating scent of rich amber wraps around me, the deep bass vibrating through my bones, even the hot sticky heat radiating off of the dance floor.

Accepting his challenge, I crawl into his lap and smooth down the silky blood red fabric of my dress.

Atlas stares at me as he wraps his hands around my throat and squeezes. Not enough to cut my airflow, but enough for my heart rate to kick up a few notches. The possessiveness in his eyes sets me on fire and as he grips my jaw and tilts my head from side to side, anticipation builds inside of me.

"What the fuck am I going to do with you?" He asks, looking deep into my eyes.

I visibly swallow and stare back at him. "Whatever you think is best."

"Mmm." Atlas groans, sliding his hand down my throat before pausing at the center of my chest. "Good answer, Kitten."

He runs his fingers up and down the plunging neckline of my dress and it feels like my chest is going to explode. It's a harmless touch, but everything about the way he's looking at me feels so innately sexual that just having his hands on me feels provocative.

"You, in this," he whispers, pulling me close as he swipes his tongue out to moisten his lips, "the sexiest fucking thing

I've ever seen." He lets out a deep breath and presses his lips to my ear. "It's a shame I plan to rip it off of you tonight." Atlas hooks his finger under my chin and pulls me in for a provocative kiss.

The kiss starts soft, sensuous even, but quickly grows dirtier as the heat between us builds. Atlas slides his hand to the back of my head and gathers my hair into a tight fist. He tugs slightly, and the sweet pain causes a little moan to slip from my lips. I feel him groan in my mouth and I readjust on his lap so we're chest to chest.

Atlas' body freezes and without warning, he breaks the kiss. My chest heaves and I search his eyes for some kind of explanation. *What the hell, we were just getting started?*

"As much as I'd love to continue," He says, pressing a kiss to my forehead as his hand reaches for my chin and tilts it to my left. "We still have an unwelcome guest in our midst."

My eyes flash to the server and see the unmistakable look of desire in her eyes as her entire face turns bright red.

"Pride is the crutch of the insecure." Atlas says, speaking to her but never taking his eyes off of me. "My queen is being gracious enough to give you a second chance. Take it."

I press my lips into the crook of his neck and try to hide my smile as she clumsily stomps away.

"I can't believe she stayed to watch." I say, pulling back to look him in the eyes.

Atlas smiles. "Can't say that I blame her." He says, staring at my flushed lips. "Besides, she wasn't the only one watching."

Atlas flashes his eyes toward the crowd and it clicks. Hell's Tavern is deceptively dark and with the music pumping and the faces around us cast in darkness, it's easy to forget we aren't alone.

"Should we head home and finish what we started?"

"I have a better idea." I say, dipping my hand between us and rubbing his hard length through his pants. "We wanted to make an impression. How about we give them a show none of them will ever forget?"

Before I can change my mind, and before he can try to talk me out of it. I stand up in front of him and make a show of tying my hair up. "My only question is, are you in?"

"As you wish, my queen." Atlas stretches out his arms along the back of the sofa and flashes me a wicked smile.

Kneeling in front of him, I run my hands up and down his tree-trunk thighs and unzip his fly.

"You sure you want to do this, Kitten?" He asks, rubbing his thumb against my jaw.

I reach for his impressive cock and rub my thumb over the drop of pre-cum already forming at the tip. "I've never been more sure about anything." I say, smiling up at him. Atlas' golden brown eyes are blown with desire and seeing the way he's staring at me only solidifies my resolve.

I lean over and guide his tip into my mouth, wincing a little at the stretch it takes to fit him all in. With my lips wrapped around his cock, I slowly glide my head up and down. Atlas groans and I move my head faster, encouraged by his sounds of pleasure.

Tears well in my eyes as I take him in deeper, but I don't back down. I keep taking him deeper and deeper. His huge cock rams against the back of my throat and I instinctively jerk back, releasing him with a loud pop. I look up at Atlas, and his expression changes from concern to hunger the second he realizes I'm going back for more. I take his cock in again and this time; I glide my mouth up and down the length of his cock shamelessly.

It's messy and drool dribbles down his shaft, but it only seems to turn him on more. His hands reach for the back of my head and he begins guiding my movements. Showing me how deep and how fast he wants it as his hips jut forward. He grits his teeth and groans as I work his massive cock, and despite having all the attention on him, I can already feel my wetness pooling.

It's such a turn on to know he's losing all of his composure because of me. To know that even-though I'm choking on his cock, I'm the one with the power and he's the one at my mercy. He lets out an audible curse and, without warning, he jerks my head away from his cock.

My lips release his tip with a pop, and I flash him a wide smile. "Too much?" I ask, staring up at him through my lashes.

"Not nearly enough." He grunts, pulling me up to my feet.

His hands wrap around my thighs and slowly inch their way up. I feel a sharp tug and before I know it; he rips my thong off of my body. Atlas flashes me a wicked grin as he crumples the black cloth and discretely tucks it into his suit jacket. His movements are quick, so lightning fast and precise, I doubt anyone else in the room knows what's going on.

Atlas looks up at my face. "Well, Kitten?" He asks, moving his hands behind my knees. "Ready for the grande finale?"

"You want them to watch." I note, narrowing my eyes at the anomaly sitting in front of me as I fight the urge to smile.

It's hard to believe that a few weeks ago, both he and I were denying our feelings for each other. We loved each other from afar for years and it's strange to think now, in front of a room of people, at Hell's Tavern of all places, our story is coming full circle.

"Maybe I do." He says, pulling my knees in to straddle the sides of his hips. "You're my queen. I want every person in this room to see who has, and who will always belong to me." To finish his proclamation, Atlas slides his tongue up the center of chest and smirks, leaving me feeling a little lightheaded and delirious.

As crazy as it seems, something inside of me wants to be seen. To be possessed. To be claimed in front of a room full of strangers. To finally feel like I'm not alone, even if just for a moment.

I lower myself onto his cock and the sensation is almost too much to bear. He fills me so brilliantly, so fucking completely that taking all of him in feels otherworldly. Like there's no possible way a cock can make me feel this good. I slide up his shaft slightly as we look into each other's eyes and I groan.

Atlas pulls my mouth to his in a sensual kiss as he wraps his large hands around my waist. He slowly slides my pussy up and down his shaft, watching my reaction as I take in every inch of him. His strokes become more and more intense, and before I know it, he's mercilessly pounding into me.

Atlas fucks me like he's trying to resuscitate me. Like I'm on my deathbed and his cock is the only thing that can bring me back to life.

We fall into a steady rhythm with Atlas' hips jutting forward and my hips grinding against him. I can feel the eyes on us now, and it feels so fucking good to stake our claims on each other in front of everyone.

Atlas' control is fracturing right before my eyes and as he jams his cock deeper and deeper inside of me, my feverish body trembles on top of him and I feel myself come apart all over him. I cry out, but Atlas covers my mouth with his and brutally slams into me as he experiences a climax of his own.

Once we finally catch our breath and I'm able to form full sentences, I climb off him, smooth my dress down and retake my seat next to him as if nothing happened. Atlas stares at me with a mixture of unreadable emotions crossing his face.

"What?" I ask, cocking my brow. "Is there something on my face?"

Atlas lets out a little chuckle. "No." He says, looking down to pick up his drink off of the coffee table. "You just surprised me." His eyes flick up and he studies my face with pure abandon.

"Why?" I ask, with a smile. "Because I didn't go completely ape-shit on her? Or because I let you fuck me in the middle of your club."

Atlas smiles and I stare at the faint little crinkles starting to form in the corner of his eyes. "A little of both." He says, chuckling to himself. "I'm impressed."

I nod my head in agreement. "I think I'm finally learning that fighting doesn't solve everything. I mean it can, temporarily. But in the long run, you can't keep doing the same shit and expect a different outcome."

"And what kind of outcome are you looking for?"

"I don't know." I say honestly. "As a kid, I always wanted my life to be like a fairytale. To find my prince and have a fairytale ending. But I think I gave up on having a happily ever after a long time ago."

"That's fair." He says, taking a sip of his drink. "Life has a way of altering plans and changing perspectives when we least expect it. What about now?"

"Now, I just want to be happy. For however long that lasts."

"Do you think you'll ever find that with me?" He asks, looking up at me through his dark lashes. The vulnerability I see in his eyes punches me in the gut. He's putting himself out there, while I'm still guarding my feelings like my life depends on it.

"Forget I asked." He says, setting his drink down to stand up. "It doesn't matter."

He's right. It doesn't matter. I'm stuck with The Reapers whether I want to be or not. But at least I know that for Atlas Cole, my happiness means something to him.

SEVENTEEN

Stevie

Goosebumps form across my skin as the shower kicks on and hot steam fills the air. I close my eyes and dip my head under the stream, letting the heavy droplets crash against me. It's almost cathartic. The way the water seems to wash everything away. All of my sins. All of my mistakes. Everything.

Alex is dead. That thought alone used to send me spiraling, but with each passing day, it's getting easier and easier to stomach the notion. I don't know for sure. No one does. But if

I let myself believe it, maybe it'll be easier to accept when I finally get the news.

Telling myself she's dead is a powerful tool. It makes me colder. More numb. Someone who has nothing to lose. It makes me stronger. More ruthless. Scarier than I ever thought I'd be. It offers me the finality I need. The kind that changes people and turns them into monsters.

It's been two weeks since Alex's kidnapping. Two weeks of radio silence from the people that took her, and two weeks of feeling myself slowly descend into madness. Nothing has changed. Even Creed's Mercenaries are quiet now. They stopped checking in a week ago after they realized every call was only setting us up for disappointment.

It's like she's vanished. Up and left, leaving no trace of her behind. Though they'll never outright say it, everyone else in this house has long given up on the idea of finding her alive. They've accepted her fate and have been able to move on with their lives. In some ways, I envy them for it. No matter how much I try to convince myself she's gone, I'll never be able to move on or accept it. Not until I know for sure.

The first night of staking out Hell's Tavern ended up being a bust. Aside from ruffling a few feathers, we didn't find anything substantial to help us find her.

Since then, I've been visiting the club almost every night. Sometimes with Atlas, sometimes with one of the twins, and sometimes alone. Ezra vanished too. He still lives here. I see evidence of his presence from time to time, but as far as he and I are concerned, he may as well be missing, too. The pain of losing him would probably hurt a lot worse if the cut from Alex's kidnapping weren't so deep.

I shut off the nozzle, step out of the shower, and wrap

myself up in a soft white towel. Bracing myself against the black granite countertop, I mentally prepare myself to look up. I haven't been able to look at myself in days, partially because I don't care what I look like anymore, and partially because I fear who I'll see staring back at me. But enough is enough, and it's time for me to stop being a coward.

I slowly raise my gaze, lingering on the sleek metal faucet before traveling up to the illuminated edge of the mirror. *You can do this.* I visibly swallow and shake my head before releasing a sigh. Quick and easy, Stevie. I flick my eyes up and let out an audible gasp at the sight in front of me.

I'm there, looking just as haggard as I expected, but just beyond me, there's a large figure shrouded in darkness, staring back at me. The hood he's wearing obscures most of his features, but as he slowly tilts his chin up, recognition clicks.

"Jesus Ezra," I snap, flipping my body around to face him, "you scared the shit out of me."

"Yeah." He says, shrugging his shoulders. "I tend to do that."

"Why are you in here?"

His eyes flash to the vanity before settling back on me. "I need some supplies and got tired of waiting."

I awkwardly shuffle to the side and study him as he shakes off his hood and steps up to the vanity I was just blocking. Without the shield of his hood, I see that he's hurt. If the deep cut over his right brow doesn't give it away, the slight limp in his walk does.

"What happened to you?" I ask as he raids through the first-aid drawers.

Ezra doesn't bat an eye at my question.

"Nothing for you to concern yourself with." He says, reaching for the bottle of liquid band-aid. There are fresh cuts on his swollen knuckles, and though he doesn't say so, both of his hands look like they're broken.

"Let me help." I say, gently removing the bottle from his battered hands.

Ezra says nothing to stop me, so I hop up on the counter and pull both of his hands into my lap.

"You want to tell me what's going on with you?" I ask, ripping an alcohol pad pack open to clean his cuts.

"I'm good."

"I'm sorry." I sputter, keeping my eyes on his hands as I bring up the conversation we've both been avoiding. "I shouldn't have said you were damaged beyond repair. I was angry and I was willing to say anything to fight back."

Ezra clenches his jaw as he audibly exhales. "You were calling it like it is." He says, keeping his eyes low. "One perk of being as fucked up as I am is I can tell when someone is lying. You weren't."

"That's not true." I say, hopping down from the counter to try to get him to look me in the eye.

Ezra makes a move to leave, but I throw myself between him and the door.

"It's been fun, Angel. Truly." He hisses, narrowing his eyes at me. "Now kindly get out of my way."

"N-no." I stammer, shaking my head. "If you're going to go back out there, you're going to get yourself killed."

"Trust me. Out there, I'm the predator. Never the prey. This is nothing compared to the damage I inflict."

"I'm not letting you leave." I say, moving between him and the door.

He lets out a dark laugh before looking down at me. "What are you going to do?" He challenges, stepping closer. "Are you going to try to stop me, Angel?"

His voice is menacing, and the cold, calculated way he's staring at me reminds me so much of the first night we met. Of how much he used to terrify me. He and I have come so far since then and I refuse to let the Ezra I know just slip away. Without thinking, I lunge for the knife sticking out of the holster on his hip and hold it up against him. I won't attack him, but he doesn't know that.

"You think taking my knife will protect you? I could kill you with my bare hands, Angel. Snap that pretty little neck of yours so quickly you won't even feel it."

"You wouldn't."

"Oh, but I would. And the sad thing is, there wouldn't even be any repercussions for me. We wouldn't even have to hide the body. After all, no one would come looking for you. No one would care. You'd be just as insignificant as your dead little sister."

"Shut up." I scream, shaking my head. "Just shut the fuck up!"

"Maybe I should kill you. Then you two can finally reunite, just like you always wanted."

He steps closer, forcing the blade against his throat. I try to back away towards the vanity, but his footsteps seem to follow mine.

"Do it." He taunts. "Now's your only chance. I'm unhinged. Two seconds away from killing you and every person you've ever cared about. If you're smart, you'll eliminate the threat now."

I stare at him for a few seconds as I try to still my quivering hand.

Ezra laughs. "You think you're a match for me, but you're wrong. You don't crave pain the same way that I do. You don't even have it in you to hurt me. You and I are nothing alike."

"You're wrong." I say, pressing the knife into his skin deep enough to draw blood. "I can be just as brutal to protect the ones I love. And whether or not you want to accept it, you are someone I love."

"You shouldn't love someone like me." He says, inching his body closer until the hard edge of vanity bites into my lower back.

I squeeze the base of the knife tighter as I watch the blood slowly seep down the blade.

"I'm a dangerous man." He says, gently wrapping his hand around my trembling wrist. His touch is soft, tender even, and the resistance inside of me starts to slip. I shake my head in a feeble attempt to keep focused, but his smoky grey eyes lock onto mine and I sink into their inky depths as everything else melts away.

"I'll hurt you." He growls, yanking my wrist down and painfully twisting it behind my body. The sharp knife slips from my fingers and crashes onto the vanity as he forces me to turn around to stop my arm from snapping.

"I'll use you." He says, gripping my hair and forcing me to bend over as he retrieves his knife.

He presses my face against the cold granite, and I almost want to cry. Not because I'm scared, but because this is the first time I've felt anything in days.

"Is this what you want?" He hisses, gripping the back of

my neck in a painful sign of possession as his fingers dig into my flesh. "You want to feel my monster?"

Yes. I want to scream, but I hold back, not wanting anything to change whatever this is that's building between us. This is what I needed. I needed him.

"This." He says, ripping the towel off of my body and leaving me bare and exposed. "This is who I really am. I don't ask, I take. I don't build, I destroy. I don't fix, I break."

Using his knife, Ezra scratches a long line from the nape of my neck down to the top of my ass, leaving a trail of goosebumps in his wake. My body trembles and I visibly flinch as he slams the knife down on the granite, mere inches from my face.

"I've shielded you from this." He taunts, yanking off his belt and kicking off his jeans and boxers. "Because I wanted to be different for you. But I'll never change and it's time you see me for who I really am. A fucking monster."

He releases my head and his fingers bite into my hips with a bruising grip. He doesn't ease into me. He kicks my legs apart, licks his fingers and sweeps his hand from the top of my clit down to my ass. He isn't gentle or kind. He places his cock at my entrance, and without warning, slams into me with so much intensity that my body keels over.

"Fuck." I groan, trying to scramble up to my elbows as my body lurches forward from his erratic thrusts. The sudden fullness is equally as pleasurable as it is painful and my body writhes beneath him as I experience a storm of sensations.

"You summoned the monster, Angel." He hisses, pounding his enormous cock into me mercilessly. "Now this tight little pussy belongs to him."

Sweat coats my skin as every touch sets my body on fire.

It's too good. The angry strokes, the dangerous possessiveness, even the sound of his powerful hips slapping my ass is sending me over the edge.

My body trembles as an orgasm builds within me. Suddenly, I want him to see what he's doing to me. I want him to know just how good it feels to have him inside of me. To watch his reaction as I come all over his cock. To know that despite what he thinks, I can take whatever his monster throws my way.

I move up from my elbows and shift my weight to the palms of my hands. From this new position, I can see Ezra in all of his beautiful glory. He's naked too and his entire body is coated with a light sheen of sweat, making every hard line on his body radiate under the light. I watch him for a moment as all the lust, anger, and possessiveness explodes out of him. He grips my hips tighter and his eyes stare mesmerized at the crux of where his cock meets my pussy. Then, as if he senses I'm watching, his eyes flicker up and I immediately implode.

Stars burst behind my eyes as I grind against his cock and savor each delicious stroke he throws my way. I'm coming apart and I'm milking his cock like my life depends on it.

I blink my eyes open and search for his eyes in the mirror. There they are. The hazy grey orbs with the power to emote so much and make me feel so many things. We lock eyes and Ezra sees the effect he has on me, at the same moment I see the effect I have on him. It's too much for either of us to handle. As we reach the peak of our impossible high, he flashes me a wicked grin and I brace my hand against the mirror, preparing for the pounding of a lifetime.

The second my skin touches the glass, his smile falters

and before I even realize what's happening, the fullness I feel inside of me vanishes.

The severance is so out of the blue, so jarring that for a second I just stand there squeezing my eyes shut, giving my body time to mourn the loss. When I'm ready to speak again, I blink my eyes open and find the bathroom completely empty.

For a second, I stand there questioning my sanity. *Did I just imagine that whole scenario?* I glance around the room in disbelief, seeing no traces of Ezra in sight.

I turn back around to face the sink, and the pieces of the puzzle click together. He was here. The black pocket knife he left on the counter proves it. I pick it up and close it, gripping it tightly in my hands.

What the hell happened? My eyes travel up to stare at my reflection, and that's when I see it. The bloody handprint I must've left on the mirror. Fuck. I cut myself earlier without realizing it and the blood must have sobered him up. *Goddamnit, Ezra.*

Ezra was right about one thing. He is a monster. But he's my monster and I wouldn't want him any other way.

EIGHTEEN

Stevie

My bare thigh peels from the leather barstool as I cross and uncross my legs. After putting in my order, I swivel around and begin searching the crowd. Jaime, my regular bartender, garnishes my water with a lime before popping a black straw in and sliding the glass towards me. "Thanks." I offer, picking it up without giving him so much as a glance. By now he knows it's nothing personal. I'm here on a mission and I need to stay focused, so alcohol and socializing are strictly off-limits.

I've gotten better at this. At studying the facial cues of strangers. Surface emotions were always the easiest to decipher. We willingly express things like happiness, anger, and excitement because those are the emotions we want surrounding people to feel.

But the hidden ones are harder to grasp. Things like sadness, deceit, and fear. When it comes to those emotions, we stop at nothing to protect them. To stuff them down, so they never see the light of day. But no matter how good of a poker face we think we have, every single person has a tell. It's usually something small. A twitch in the face. A shift in the eyes. Something physical that hints at the truth just clawing to get out.

That's what I'm looking for as I lock eyes with these strangers. A flicker of recognition followed by a telltale sign of fear. It's a tiring job, and a lot of the time, I feel like all of this work is getting me nowhere. But this is the one thing that I can do to help find my sister. The one slice of control I have left in the chaos that's become my life.

"Where are your men tonight?"

At first I mistook the man walking up to me as a stranger, but after hearing him speak, the tinge of a Russian accent is a dead giveaway. *Dimitri.* I flick my eyes to my right and give him a quick glance. "Close." I deadpan, wanting him to feel every ounce of the threat in my tone. Atlas left thirty minutes ago to meet up with one of their contacts uptown, but he doesn't need to know that. "What do you want?"

Dimitri nods his head as a hint of a smile forms on his lips. "I've been watching you, Kroshka." Dimitri says, sitting on the barstool next to me. "At first, I wrote it off as coincidental, but after seeing you sitting in this very spot for almost a week now, I know what you're doing."

"I don't know what you're talking about." I bluff, wrapping my arms across my chest.

"You do." Dimitri insists, swiveling the drink in his hand before tossing it back. "Of this, I'm sure. It's a valiant effort, though ultimately pointless. Your sister's killer would never show their face here."

"She's not dead." I snap, glaring up at him as I feel the rage build within me. "God. Why am I even bothering to argue with you? I'm not doing anything but having a drink at my favorite bar."

"So then, it's just a coincidence that you've been here every night for the last week?" He presses. "Why is it that when you're here, you choose this exact seat every time? It's the only seat on the bar that gives visibility of the entire club. All of that is simply a coincidence?"

"Yeah." I retort. "It is."

Dimitri takes a seat on the barstool next to me and I bristle. "If you want my opinion—"

"I don't." I say, cutting him off.

"Well, I'm feeling generous, so I'll give it anyway. You're looking in the wrong direction. Whoever took your sister did so to get to you. To get under your skin. It's why you haven't found her yet. As I understand it, there's still one person your men haven't questioned that vehemently hates you. The same person who used to manage this very bar."

Either I'm going crazy, or everything Dimitri's saying is making a lot of sense. Clenching my jaw, I look to the side and I glare at him. Studying his expression to see if he's telling me the truth.

"If I were them," he continues, "she would have been my first stop. Then again, your men have always been strangely attached to her. Perhaps nostalgia has them sparing her from your wrath."

"I considered Jessie…" I say, trailing off. "But they said it was impossible. That she wouldn't have the power or the means to do it."

The truth has been right in front of my face all along. *It's Jessie*. It has to be Jessie. They eliminated her as a suspect right off the bat, and I was stupid enough to go along with it. I trusted them, and they betrayed me to spare someone they always considered as one of their own.

Dimitri stares at me for a moment before continuing and the look in his eyes is one of pure pity. He feels sorry for me. How fucking sick and twisted is it that a man who assaulted me is the only one willing to help me figure out the truth?

"As I understand it," he continues, gauging my reaction, "they underestimated her once before and, in doing so, nearly got you killed. Who's to say history isn't repeating itself?"

I blink back the tears forming in my eyes and visibly swallow. I refuse to cry. Not again, and especially not because of their betrayal.

"They would never let me question her." I say, staring at the floor numbly as my world caves in. "Even if I confronted them now, I know they wouldn't."

"I could arrange that." Dimitri says, leaning forward to touch my forearm in a kind gesture. "We could head there now and you can get the answers you seek."

"Why would you help me?" I ask, turning in my seat to face him. "What do you get out of all this?" There has to be something else in this for him. Something beyond helping me for the greater good. After our first fucked-up interaction, he's been relatively kind to me, but that doesn't make him a good guy.

"Think of it as my penance for my transgressions against you. I am sorry for my actions and hopefully helping you will prove that."

I don't believe for one second Dimitri's intentions are purely altruistic. But we haven't gotten a genuine lead in weeks. He's cornered me alone so many times in the last few weeks that if he truly wanted to hurt me again, he would've. *Maybe a part of him does regret what happened.*

"Let's go." I say, glaring up at him. "But I'm driving myself."

Tristan left the keys to his Maserati here on the off chance something came up. I'd argue that this "something" warranted a drive and frankly, I still don't trust Dimitri enough to be in a car alone with him.

Jessie's in jail, but that doesn't mean she couldn't have orchestrated Alex's kidnapping. She'd orchestrated worse in the past, and that was before she had an actual reason to hate me.

AFTER SLIPPING out of Hell's Tavern in Tristan's black Maserati, I follow Dimitri through the busy streets of Downtown and make my way to Jessie's new home, The Caspian County Correctional Facility. It's nearly 1 AM, but the center of the city is still very much alive and buzzing. Neon lights, packed clubs, and late nite eateries line the entire main strip. We pull up to a red light and I can't help but stare at the young people dancing and laughing in the streets. They look like they're having the time of their life and a small pang of jealousy hits me in the stomach. *That could easily be me in another life.*

The light turns green and as my car moves forward, so do I. There's no point in thinking about the "what if's". I'm not like those kids back there, and thanks to the hand life dealt me, I never will be.

After a few minutes, Dimitri leads us onto a random street far from the road. The tiny alleyway we pull into is sandwiched between two tall buildings and is barely wide enough to fit a car. There isn't a streetlight in sight and as Dimitri's car gets swallowed by the darkness, I can't shake the ominous feeling in my bones. Everything about this feels wrong.

Dimitri pulls his car to stop at the end of the alley and casually steps out. He waits for a few seconds for me to do the same, but when he spots my hesitation, he walks over to my driver's side window.

"Are you planning on getting out?" He asks, crouching down to level his eyes on me.

"Yes." I answer, glaring up at him. I visibly swallow and stare out at the sign posted in front of the building to our right. Caspian County Correctional Facility. I can't believe I'm here. *What the hell am I doing?*

"If you don't want to do this," he offers, "we can go back. My contact will understand."

"No. Let's go. I'm just going to ask her some questions, there's nothing wrong with that."

I'm telling the truth, but it feels like a lie as it slips

through my lips. In the back of my mind, I know The Reapers would hate this. Would hate that I've gone behind their back and done this without them.

But it's been over three weeks and I'm no closer to finding my sister, if The Reapers are really helping me, like they swear they are. We should've found her by now. Dimitri may be an asshole, but he's the only one willing to help me.

I step out of the car and dig my heels firmly into the pavement. Dimitri smiles and leads the way to a nondescript door on the side of the building. He knocks on the cool metal three times in succession, and takes a step back, waiting for an answer.

Within seconds, the door glides open and a portly man in his mid-50s opens the door. He's dressed in a light brown suit with a holster on his hip. His eyes move from me to Dimitri before giving him a glare. "You were supposed to come alone." He says, looking down at me pointedly.

"Change of plans." Dimitri offers back.

"Fine." The man says, running his hand down his face. "But I want the blackmailing to stop. I've done enough favors for you, Evanoff. I'm done being your puppet."

Dimitri flashes the man a smile that's anything but friendly, and slowly shakes his head. "Poor Robert. You're done when I say you're done. Now please, kindly escort me and my lovely guest inside."

He said please, but there was no hint of politeness in his tone. It's a demand laced with a threat. The man clenches his jaw and steps aside to allow the two of us entry. After unlocking a metal gate and sliding it aside, he leads us down a narrow corridor lined with pale blue walls and dark gray floors. The space smells of potent chemical cleaner and something else that I can't quite place. Something putrid that makes my skin crawl.

"You'll have 10 minutes with her, tops." The officer growls as he unlocks another gate. "I've sent the guard on duty out on an errand. Make your questions quick and don't leave any evidence that you were here."

"Thank you kindly, Sheriff." Dimitri says, giving him a mocking salute.

"Yeah." The man scoffs, pocketing his keys as he turns to leave. "You know, The Reapers and I have always been on opposite sides of the law. They corrupt my men, and I arrest theirs. But they've never once stooped as low as you have. You're threatening my family. My life. And some wrongs can never be made right."

"Is that a threat, Sheriff Winston?" Dimitri asks, sounding way more delighted than he should.

"Just an observation, kid. I've been in the underbelly of this city for a long time and I've learned a few things. All things must learn to co-exist if they want to survive."

"Survival is for the weak." Dimitri retorts, sliding the door open and gesturing for me to enter. "Time is ticking. Why don't you go make yourself useful and grab the girl?"

The Sheriff glares at Dimitri for a few seconds, as if debating on whether or not to say more. Deciding that the conversation is done, he sets off to go retrieve Jessie.

After he leaves, Dimitri and I take our seats on one side of the metal table, leaving a single chair for Jessie on the other.

"I thought you said he was a friend." I say, glaring at Dimitri.

"There are no real friends in this world, Kroshka, only tools. Pliable & resourceful, designed to make our lives easier.

But ultimately, you can't trust them. They'll break in the end. They always do."

"Nice outlook."

"And yours is much better?" He retorts. "Remind me, why didn't you want to loop your men in on what we're doing right now?"

"That's different." I say, shaking my head. "My sister is in danger."

"But you're close to them, are you not? Sounds like two sides of the same coin to me."

I narrow my eyes at him as a smug smirk forms on his face.

"You know what?" I say, crossing my arms over my chest. "You can leave. I'm in the building, and I definitely no longer need your help."

Dimitri laughs at the obvious annoyance in my tone. "Add miss all the action? Never."

"Fine. Then can you just stay quiet? I need to think about what I'm going to ask her and your constant babbling isn't helping."

Dimitri pretends to zip his lips shut and I let out a shaky breath. I don't have time to think about the repercussions of this visit, or what it could mean for my relationship with The Reapers. This isn't an about them, it's about Alex and if talking to Jessie can help me find my sister, I'm going to fucking do it whether they like it or not.

NINETEEN

I HEAR THE SOUND OF APPROACHING FOOTSTEPS AND MY stomach dips. *This is it.* I'm coming face-to-face with the woman who nearly killed me and could be the one responsible for taking my sister. I flick my eyes up as she enters the room and see her mood shift the second she locks eyes with me.

"What the fuck is this?" She asks, glaring back at the sheriff who ushered her in.

"These two have a few questions for you." He says, shoving her forward. "Don't do anything stupid, and you'll go back to your cell in one piece." With that, the sheriff backs out of the room and shuts the door behind him.

Jessie stands in the corner of the room and stares at us. Her eyes flick from me to Dimitri, then back to me.

"My, my, my..." She says, slowly shaking her head. "Look who we have here. What an unexpected pairing."

"Sit." I order, glaring at her as I gesture to the empty chair. Time is of the essence, and I refuse to waste any of it playing into her mind games. She isn't the one in control here. I am.

Jessie slides the metal chair out and takes a seat across from us. She levels her eyes on us and it's the first time I'm able to get a really good look at her. She looks like hell. Her once shiny, wavy hair is now wild and frayed. Her once vivid eyes are dull and lifeless, lacking all the emotion they used to have. Her skin is different too, bruised, sullen, and littered with fresh scars. *Looks like she's made some enemies here, too.* For a second, I almost feel sorry for her. Fighting for your life in a cage is no way to live. Then I remember why we're here, and just like that, my sympathy vanishes. She deserves everything she's had to endure, and then some.

Jessie rests her hands on the table and my eyes flick to metal cuffs securely fastened around them. "Like what you see?" She taunts, noticing me staring. "They're on my ankles too, in case you're worried I'll finish what I started."

"I doubt you'd be so stupid." Dimitri notes, leaning back in his seat. "But if you try to hurt her, you won't live very long to enjoy it." Jessie's eyes flicker from him to me and a smug smile spreads across her face.

"Wow." She says, stifling a laugh as she shakes her head. "You're fucking him."

Heat rushes up my neck as I feel Jessie's pointed glare

burn into my skin. The accusation in her eyes is ridiculous. There's nothing going on between me and Dimitri besides some weird mutual understanding. *That's it.*

"Do The Reapers know?" She presses.

"What? No. I mean —" I hesitate and her green eyes light up. "No. There's nothing going on between us. Not that it's any of your business."

Jessie smirks at me. "Whatever you say, Pet."

"Time is almost up." Dimitri chimes in. "Get to the point."

"Look, I came here to ask you about my sister."

"Sweet little Alex?" She asks, flashing me a smile. "How is she, by the way?"

The way she asks the question feels off. Like she knows a lot more about Alex than she's letting on.

"Why don't you tell me?" I ask, narrowing my eyes at her.

She cocks her head and glares at me, but says nothing.

"Enough with the games Jessie." I hiss, slamming my palm against the metal table. "I know you're lying through you fucking teeth. I don't know how you pulled it off, but I know you're the one who took her."

Jessie doesn't deny the allegations, so I continue. "It's never a crime to steal from a thief? I got the message you left loud and clear. I took your family, so you took mine."

Jessie just stares at me.

"Look, it's not too late to fix this." I add. "If you end this now, I'll talk to The Reapers and try to get them to forgive you. Just give her back to me."

Jessie pauses for a moment and studies my face. Maybe my words are reaching her. Maybe she wants to make this right.

"It looks like we're both shit out of luck." She says, sitting up higher in her chair. "Because giving her back is the one thing I can't do, not unless you have a time machine."

My heart falls to the pit of my stomach as I stare at her unflinchingly. *She took her.* "What do you mean?" I ask, peering into her soulless green eyes. "Why can't you give her back?"

"She's dead." She deadpans, smirking at me. "I killed her hours before I nearly killed you."

All the air in my lungs rushes out as I stare at her in disbelief. "No." I say, shaking my head. "You said you let her go. You said you broke her phone and let her leave."

"God Stevie, you're so fucking naïve." She scoffs, sliding her hands to her lap. "I lied. I thought I was doing you a favor by sparing you the truth. You were going to die, anyway."

"You're lying." I spit through my gritted teeth. She's just trying to fuck with my head. The takeout containers were fresh. And what about the message on the glass?

"I wish I was." She presses on, casually shrugging her shoulders. "It's sad, really. It wasn't a peaceful death and the poor thing never saw it coming. But you want to know what the saddest part was?" Jessie asks, leaning forward in her seat. "While I watched my men rape her over and over again, she never once cried out for help. Never begged for someone to make it stop. That was surprising, but I guess she knew no one would come to her rescue. I mean, even her own sister was too preoccupied to help."

"Liar!" I scream, shooting up from my seat.

Dimitri wraps his hand around my elbow to stop me from moving any further. "Relax." He says, trying to pull me back to my seat. "You're playing right into her game."

I shake my head indignantly and pull out of his grip. "No.

I'm not. I know she's lying. Everything she's saying is impossible."

"You're right." Jessie taunts, inching her face closer to mine. "Someone is lying, but it isn't me. Why would I lie? I have nothing left to lose. I watched her die. Saw her take her last fucking breaths. It was kind of pathetic, really."

"Stop fucking lying!" I scream, pressing my hands against my head. This is all too much. There's no way Alex died that night. There's just no fucking way. Tears well in my eyes and I don't even bother trying to stop them. Alex can't be dead. She just fucking can't be.

Jessie laughs, and the sound of her heartless cackle causes something inside of me to snap.

I leap across the table and pounce on her. My body slams against hers and we both fall to the floor with a loud thud. Wasting no time, I climb on her chest and wrap my hands around her throat, stopping her laugh in its tracks. Jessie smiles at me, and it only makes me want to squeeze her throat tighter. This is all a fucking game to her.

Squeezing her throat tighter, I jerk her head up and slam it back down. If she doesn't want to tell me the truth, maybe I can beat it out of her. With her arms and legs still cuffed, Jessie is powerless to fight back. "Tell me the truth!" I scream, smashing her head against the floor again. She winces, but the gurgling laugh doesn't stop. It only grows louder.

"I have." Jessie croaks, flashing me a mocking smile even as her face is turning bright red. "You just refuse to accept it." I release her throat and Jessie gasps, greedily pulling more air into her lungs. *This bitch is absolutely unhinged.*

Dimitri steps forward and crouches down beside me. "She

isn't scared, Kroshka." He says, gripping her chin in his hand. "Look at her. Mocking you. Openly laughing about killing your sister."

"She's lying." I hiss, staring back at him. "Alex is alive, and she knows something. She's covering for someone."

"Get the truth out of her." He says, pulling a knife from his pocket and sliding it to me. "Make her tell you everything."

I look down at Jessie and for the first time tonight; I see the look of fear in her eyes. He's right. She wasn't scared of me, that's why she didn't take my threat seriously, but thanks to the knife in my hand, she is now.

I dig my knees into her shoulders and press the icy blade against her throat. She whimpers and tries to wiggle out of my hold, but Dimitri grabs a hold of her legs and the fight within her dies. "Give me one good reason I shouldn't slit your fucking throat right now." I hiss, looming over her.

"I didn't kill her!" She exclaims, her chest heaving as tears well in her eyes. "I swear. I didn't. I was fucking with you."

Her words reek of desperation, but I finally feel the sincerity in them. Tears stream down her face as her desperate sob turns hysterical.

As pathetic as she looks, I don't feel bad for her. She caused this, caused all of this. She lied to get a rise out of me and she should suffer for it.

"Where the fuck is she?" I hiss, digging the blade into her neck. It would be so easy to kill her. The knife is insanely sharp and even slight pressure will make it slide through her skin like butter.

Jessie flinches, and a trickle of blood seeps down her

neck. "I don't know." She wails, trembling underneath me. "I swear to god, I don't know anything."

"Liar! You know something." I scream, sinking the blade even deeper into her skin. More blood is seeping down her neck, but I don't care. Even if she doesn't know anything. I want her pain, I want her blood, and I want her fear. "Tell me what you know or so help me god —"

My words get cut short as the door crashes open and I see at least three sets of legs enter the room. *Fuck.* Time's up.

I move to climb off of her, but before I can, I feel someone behind me yank me to my feet and painfully twist my wrist, forcing my knife to fall to the floor. Everything turns into chaos around me as the other voices around me rise, but it isn't until I hear one distinct voice call out from the chaos that I realize just how fucked I am.

"Get her the fuck out of here." Cyrus yells, glaring at me as he tends to Jessie's throat. "Now."

I assume he's talking to Dimitri and I lock eyes with him for a brief second before a large chest blocks my view. *Tristan.* Tristan picks me up and roughly throws me over his shoulder. I don't want to leave yet, but I can feel the anger radiating off of him, and I can't bring myself to say anything to him. There's nothing I can say.

As he pulls me from the room, my eyes linger on Jessie. She's not moving, and the blood pooling underneath her is only growing larger. *Shit. What did I do?* This is bad. This is really fucking bad.

TRISTAN THROWS me into the backseat of his Maserati and firmly slams the door. He refused to say a word to me as he escorted me out and, as he slips into the driver's seat and shuts the door, it's clear he still has nothing to say.

"How did you know where I was?" I ask, numbly staring at my stained hands. There's blood all over them. Jessie's blood.

Tristan clenches his jaw and lets out an exasperated sigh. "A t... tracker." He says, glaring at me through his rearview mirror. "All of our cars have them."

I say nothing in response. If I was thinking clearly, I would've figured as much, but everything happened so fast.

The passenger door opens, and Cyrus slides himself in before slamming the door shut behind him. He ignores my presence all together and looks at Tristan. "Did you get the text?" He asks, pulling out his cellphone.

Tristan gives him a quick nod.

"Good." Cy replies. "I spoke with Winston. He said it's fine if I leave the jeep here overnight, so we're all good. Atlas is waiting. Let's move."

Tristan throws the car in reverse and pulls us out onto the main road. We drift past the lively streets of downtown and even though I'm shuffling around in my seat, neither of them bother to give me a second glance. I'm sitting behind them, but with how distant they're acting, I may as well be on the other side of the planet.

After a few minutes of driving, I muster up the courage to speak again. "How is she?" I ask, hesitation coating every word.

"Alive." Cyrus deadpans. "Barely. No thanks to you."

"That's not fair." I say, shaking my head. "You guys weren't there. You didn't hear all the things she was saying. She was taunting me."

"Drop it, S... Stevie." Tristan orders, "just be grateful we got there in t... time."

"In time for what?" I snap, glaring at the two of them. "To stop me from getting the truth? She was about to break."

"She was about to die." Cyrus retorts, looking out at the road ahead. "She was baiting you, and it fucking worked. If you had bothered to ask us," he adds, "we would've told you questioning her was a waste of time. We've been monitoring her since her arrest. You're the only person from the outside world she's spoken to. She played no part in your sister's kidnapping."

"I d... don't get it. We ruled her out weeks ago." Tristan huffs, glaring at me through his rearview mirror. "What the f... fuck were you thinking?"

"Dimitri offered to help me with something I knew none of you would. He thought it was a good idea to question her, and I agreed."

"Don't even start trying to defend Dimitri now." Cyrus snarls, shaking his head. "He is just as in the wrong as you are."

"How?" I snap, glaring at the back of his head. "All he did was help me."

Cyrus lets out a mocking laugh before turning in his chair to stare back at me. "You honestly believe he didn't want that interaction with you and Jessie to play out just like it did? That he was only there to help you?"

"I don't know what to believe." I retort, cocking my head. "It's not like you guys keep me in the loop with anything."

"Let me give you a crash course." Cy spits, narrowing his eyes at me. "Dimitri Evanoff is the worst kind of monster. A liar and a manipulator. He preys on people's insecurities and toys with their heads for his own sick satisfaction. Assuming he's a friend is one of the stupidest things anyone can do."

I narrow my eyes at him. "You say it like you've experienced it yourself." I mumble.

"Maybe I have!" He yells, letting all the anger and frustration explode out of him. "You don't know shit about my life or what I've been through. But this is typical Stevie behavior. Quick to decide without thinking about the fucking consequences. You could've murdered someone tonight in the middle of a fucking prison. Do you not get how stupid that was?"

"At least I'm doing something to save my sister. You guys aren't doing anything! I get you don't like Dimitri, I don't either, but at least he's being proactive. The four of you could give two fucks about Alex."

"What the hell else are we supposed to do, huh?" Cyrus asks, glaring at me. "We have jobs to do, people that depend on us. We can't just stop living and throw everything aside to make you happy. We've hired the best men for the job, and have redirected a lot of our resources towards finding your sister, but you're still not happy. No. You'd rather have us out there on the streets chasing a fucking ghost."

The word *ghost* hits me in the center of my chest and I audibly gasp. A ghost. *Is that how they see Alex?*

"That's enough." Tristan warns, placing a hand on Cy's shoulder.

"No." Cyrus says, shaking his head as he lowers his voice. "It's been long enough. She needs to hear this." Cyrus reaches for my hand and squeezes it tight. "Princess, I know you've been through a lot," He says, locking eyes with me, "but these last few weeks it's like you've become a different person. Your need for violence is only getting worse, and it all circles around this idea that if you fight hard enough, you'll get your sister back. But P, no amount of bloodshed will bring her back. You almost killed Jessie back there, and to what end? Killing her wouldn't have brought your sister back. Nothing will. It's time for you to accept that Alex is gone and there's a good chance she may never come home."

"She's not gone." I say, shaking my head in denial.

"She is." He says, his voice taking on an even softer tone. "We all know it. The Mercenaries know it. Hell, even Dimitri knows it. It's why it was so easy for him to prey on you. The only person in the world who hasn't accepted that she's gone is you."

I can't believe what I'm hearing. *How could he say that? How could they all think that?* Then I realize, with startling clarity, what's really going on. *They're giving up.* On Alex, and on a search that they never *really* wanted to be a part of.

"Dimitri was right." I say, blinking back the tears welling in my eyes. "You guys don't give a shit about Alex and you never have. God, why didn't I see it? It was never in your best interest to find her. She'd take me away from you, and let's be honest, the only thing the four of you have ever cared about is yourselves."

Cyrus sighs as he runs his hands down his face. "You're

wrong." He says, before moistening his lips. "We care about you, but I'm starting to see just how stupid that is. I thought I could reason with you. That if I just talked to you, you'd wake up and see how far you've fallen from grace. But I was wrong about you. You're just another one of Dimitri's fucking puppets. Only this time, you might succeed in what the other one couldn't. All the bullshit you've pulled and all the damage you caused might actually be enough to rip this family apart."

TWENTY

Stevie

THE HOUSE IS EMPTY. EVEN WITHOUT DOUBLE CHECKING, I can tell I'm alone. It's too quiet and the air in the room is too cold.

I slip off my heels and throw them against the wall, letting out a fraction of the anger brewing inside of me. They crash against the pristine white wall with a thud and a cruel smile forms on my lips. It feels good to let it out. To be the one inflicting the damage instead of feeling it.

But once I see the black scuff marks and cracks my outburst left behind, my smile fades. *What did I do?*

I step forward and run my fingers along the cracks, as if my touch alone has the power to heal the damage. *It doesn't.* And the more I try to fix it, the more the damage spreads.

Tears well in my eyes as I step back from the wall and turn my head away. That wall is like everything else I've been doing lately. Acting on impulse only to regret it, and then try to make it better. But some things are irreparable and I'm terrified that tonight, I've finally broken the only ties I have left.

I regret how the conversation ended with Cyrus. I threw what Dimitri said in his face because I knew it would hurt him. Because everything he said was hurting me, and my instinct is always to fight fire with fire. But the reality of it is, deep down, I know Cyrus is right. Alex is gone. Dimitri can't be trusted. And I have fallen so far from grace I can't even tell which way is up.

I step through the foyer and slowly look around as I take everything in. I never really noticed it until now, but without the overwhelming presence of The Reapers filling the rooms, this house feels barren. Like nothing but grey walls, dark wood beams, and upscale fixtures. Cold. Lifeless. Deserted.

The energy in the house almost feels ironic given the current state of my mind. It's like all the dark emotions swirling inside of me poured themselves all over the house. Adorning the walls and seeping into the floors. Wreaking havoc on a place that was once a symbol for a new beginning.

I walk up the stairs in an almost catatonic state. I can feel the tears pooling in my eyes, but I don't even bother to blink them back. This isn't what I wanted. For the twins to find me like that. To see, with their own eyes, just how far I've fallen. But even our deepest darkest truths have a way of revealing themselves and mine is that I was never really the princess in my story. *I was the villain.*

I would've killed Jessie tonight. I tried to deny it in front of Cyrus and Tristan, but once they left me alone with my own thoughts, I could no longer deny the truth. And as I took the long walk up the driveway, I thought about why. *Why was I so determined to kill her?* Did I really think she knew where Alex was? Or was I just looking for an excuse to hurt her?

Then I thought about what kind of person does that. *What kind of person just kills for sport?* And when I realized the answer, I almost cried. *A monster.* A monster does that. I didn't almost kill Jessie because she was hiding information. I almost killed her because I wanted to. Because it felt good. Because I wanted her to feel a fraction of the pain I live with every fucking day. I did it because I'm a monster.

I approach the second floor landing and I have no idea where to go next. I can't stomach the idea of going into my room. Being alone in that room will surface too many emotions I'm not ready to face.

My eyes zero in on Ezra's door and I move towards it. It's probably the last place I should go, given our tumultuous last encounter, but after all this time, I still feel a pull towards his room.

I slide the door open and I inhale a deep breath as his signature scent of lavender and smoke surrounds me. *This is exactly where I need to be.*

I step in further and brush my fingers along the milky blue wall as I make a beeline for the bed. The room is pitch black with the exception of the moon casting a soft glow in the corner of the room, but I don't bother with the lights. I've done this walk countless times and know the layout of his room like the back of my hand. I find his bed and, without second guessing myself, I sink into the cloud-like mattress and feel the tension in my body ease. I need to shut myself off, even if just for a few minutes.

I AWAKE with a start at the sound of buzzing beside my head. I blink my eyes open and let out an audible groan when I realize the source, *my phone*. I must've set it on the nightstand before I drifted off.

I reach for the phone and as I lift it up; I see a small piece of paper drift to the floor. I try to grab a hold of it, but it slips through my fingers and takes a dive under the bed. Awesome.

Tossing the cozy duvet aside, I crawl out of bed and get on my hands and knees to try to find it. The second I flip up the bed skirt, the putrid scent of gasoline and ash hits my nose. *Where is that coming from?* I lift my face away from the scent and blindly reach for the paper. *It couldn't have gone too far.* I swing my hand out and my fingers latch on to two things at once. The paper that I dropped and something that feels like a pile of rough leather. I grab onto both pieces and pull them out. It's hard to see what I'm looking at with no light, so I reach for my phone and activate the flashlight.

Lifting the pile of leather in my hands, I realize almost immediately that it's a jacket. Or at least, it was. The inner lining reeks of gasoline and the exterior of the sleeves are so badly charred, it's impossible to touch it without getting soot on your hands. *What the hell is this?* I drop the pile of fabric back down to the floor and focus my attention on the paper. Now that I'm able to see it up close, I realize it isn't just a paper, it's the back of a picture.

I freeze when I see the words scribed on the back of the picture. 'Always together.' But it's not just the words that throw me off, it's the handwriting too. The handwriting I'd recognize anywhere. *Mine.*

It can't be.

I don't want to believe it, but when I flip the photo over and see two familiar faces on the other side, my world caves in on itself.

It's me and Alex. *Why the fuck does Ezra have a picture of me and Alex on his nightstand?*

My chest tightens, and suddenly there's not enough air in the room. I can't breathe and as I look around me, I know with certain clarity I need to get the fuck out of here. With only my phone in my hand, I gun it out of the room.

Vomit forces its way up my throat as I thrash through the bathroom door and the pieces of the puzzle start falling into place. The burned jacket. The picture. His absence. Everything is pointing to something I don't want to believe. *That I can't possibly believe.*

My knees crash to the floor as I brace myself over the toilet and my stomach heaves up all of its contents. My body shakes violently as nausea continues to assault me, forcing me to purge up everything as if that will somehow erase the image from my mind. He wouldn't hurt Alex. *Would he?*

Someone knocks on the door and my head snaps up. I frantically wipe my tears away as I flush down the contents of the toilet and move to my feet. I don't want any of them to see me like this. Not until I know for sure. I take a deep breath and open the door, but when I see the man behind it, my facade crumbles and all the air rushes out of my lungs.

Ezra stands on the other side of the door and stares at me. There is no sympathy in his eyes. No fear. *He knows.*

"Is she still alive?" I ask softly, blinking back the tears as they well in my eyes.

"Is who still alive?" He asks, inching closer to me.

"Don't fucking play with me, Ezra." I snap, shoving him back into the hallway. "Is. She. Still. Alive?"

Ezra scoffs as he slowly shakes his head. "That guilt you're feeling over what you did." He hisses, looking at me up and down. "Has nothing to do with me. You made your bed. Lie in it."

I narrow my eyes at him. "I'm not talking about Jessie." I spit. "I'm talking about my sister. Is she still out there somewhere, alone and scared? Or did you make it easy on yourself and just kill her?"

Ezra makes a move to respond, but I quickly cut him off. "Wait, what am I thinking?" I hiss, shaking my head. "Of course you killed her. It's who you are. You don't a give a fuck about the people you hurt or the damage you cause, all you care about is yourself."

I sink my teeth into my bottom lip as the tears pour harder. I don't care how weak I look or how much my voice shakes. After all the pain he caused, he needs to hear this. All of this. "I slept in your room today," I confess as I visibly swallow, "because I felt so broken that I thought just being closer to you would make me feel better. Isn't that fucking pathetic?"

He says nothing, so I continue. "But I see who you are so clearly now. You never healed me. You never made me feel better. You never made me feel loved. You changed me. You made me numb to your violence. You made me forget about all the things that make me human. And the fucked up thing is, I wanted so badly for you to love me that I was willing to do anything to be your equal. To show you how strong and how ruthless I could be. Just so I could walk hand in hand with your monster and show the entire world we belonged together. But you know what? I was wrong. The truth is, there's no hope for you, Ezra Cole. You're a sick, sadistic killer and no amount of love or acceptance from anyone will ever change that. I regret ever meeting you. I regret wasting my time on you. And I regret turning into the monster you always wanted me to be. "

I stare at Ezra and wait for him to respond. Part of me wants him to deny it. To grab me by shoulders, shake me, and scream that it wasn't him. That I got it all wrong and that he'll do whatever it takes to prove it. But his expression is as cold as ever and as he moves closer to me, I can almost feel the ice radiating off of him.

"You're right." He hisses, cocking his head as he slowly backs me into a wall. "I am a monster, but I've never pretended to be anything else. You're the one that thought you could change me. That I would magically transform into some prince that'll come through and save the day. But that'll never be me, and it isn't my responsibility to live up to some warped ideology of who you want me to be. You may be right about who I am and all the things I've done, but you're wrong about one thing. I never wanted you to be a monster. That you did all on your own. I've accepted the blood on my hands, Angel, your sister's included. But when the fuck are you going to accept yours?"

As soon as I hear the confession fall from his lips, I stop listening. I've heard enough and hearing anymore will only make it hurt more. Ezra walks away, leaving me alone in the hallway to deal with the damage he caused.

His door slams shut, and I sink to the floor. I wrap my arms around my knees and slowly rock myself as my tears continue to pour. *He did it.* He actually fucking did it. Ezra killed my little sister. Pain slices into me as the reality of his betrayal hits me over and over again. I trusted him. I trusted all of them. *How could I be so fucking stupid?*

I look around the hallway, and the sudden need to escape hits me hard. I don't belong here. I shake myself out of my sadness and force myself up to my feet. *No.* I think to myself, shaking the tears away. *No more crying. You've already wasted so many tears on men you barely knew. Don't let Alex's death be in vain. Get the fuck out of here now, before it's too late.*

Stuffing my emotions back down, I rush into my room, grab my duffel bag, fill it with as many necessities as I can think of, put my sneakers on, and storm right back out. If I stay any longer, it'll be even harder to leave.

I race down the stairs and head straight for the back door. After my first failed escape attempt, I figured out a better route. I never thought I'd have to use it, but it's just another sign of how drastically things have changed.

Once I make it into the backyard, I slip past the servants' quarters, scale the back access gate, and enter the lush forest surrounding the estate. There's only about two miles of trees until I hit the main highway, but the only way I'll be able to make it down the hill is with some outside help.

Shit. I can't do this alone. Pulling out my phone, I scroll through my messages to find the number I never saved. The one I thought I'd never need again.

ME: Hey. I know it's late and I'm probably the last person you want to hear from, but something happened and I have no one else to turn to. Will you help me?

As I find my way through the forest, I keep the message app open, willing for those three little grey dots to pop up. Twenty minutes pass and I've all but given up hope on getting a response. It's almost 3:30 AM, and it was dumb for me to assume they'd even want to help me again after everything that's happened. Just as I'm about to slip my phone back into my pocket, it buzzes, and a message pops up on the screen.

UNKNOWN NUMBER: Sure. Where are you?

TWENTY-ONE

Tristan

Tonight was supposed to be a quiet night, but when Dimitri's involved, it never is. After we pulled Stevie out of that fucking interrogation room, Dimitri sent Atlas a text requesting to hold a last-minute meeting at Hell's Tavern tonight. Atlas could've said no, but that would've forced us to travel to another syndicate's sanctuary. And after finding Dimitri so close to our girl, none of us were comfortable leaving her alone. Even Ezra, who's been keeping his distance, agreed to head back to the house and keep an eye on her. I still can't believe Dimitri got her in his clutches, and all four of us missed the signs.

"I can't believe you okayed this shit." Cyrus hisses, cutting his eyes at Atlas and we vacate his office and head downstairs.

Atlas says nothing in response, but the empty expression on his face speaks volumes. He doesn't want this meeting to happen any more than we do.

The three of us step onto the main floor of Hell's Tavern and it feels like we're walking into a battlefield. It's just after 4 AM and even with all of our customers gone, the air in the room feels stifling. We step towards our lounge, and it's as if every eye in the room is following us. It's fucking unnerving. We may be on home turf, but it's hard to feel completely at ease with so many killers filling our booths.

Once we reach our section, we settle into the blue velvet couches and quietly assess our company. Given the short four-hour notice, I'm surprised to see representatives of every west coast syndicate in attendance. The Immortals of Portland. The Brotherhood in San Francisco. The Devil's Disciples of Los Angeles. Even The Forsaken of Seattle made it in time.

Like us, none of them wear any obvious markers showing their affiliations, but I spot each crew's leader with no problem. Being head of security means it's my job to keep tabs on everybody, including our allies. After all, the thin line between enemy and friend often blurs in our line of business.

Everyone made it on time, but no one looks happy about it. Even Dimitri's ex-crew looks irritated. He must've not bothered to clue them in on his plans, either.

It's just after 4:20 AM when the man of the hour finally strolls in.

"Sorry to keep you waiting." Dimitri says, taking off his jacket and hanging it over a chair. "Something unexpected came up."

The way he throws a pointed glare at our table elicits a flicker of rage in all of us. If we didn't know that Ezra was watching her like a fucking hawk right now, that shit would've sent us into a frenzy.

"Thank you all for agreeing to meet on such short notice." He continues, offering everyone in the room a menacing smile. Dimitri knows none of us have a real say in the manner. If we get a text from the West Coast leader, we have no choice but to answer.

"The Reapers have been hospitable enough to offer their space as a meeting point and I want you all to know that tonight, this is a neutral space."

"Cut to the chase, Mitri." Alek, The head of The Immortals, calls out. "Where's your father and what is this all about?"

Guess we weren't the last ones to find out about Oleg's passing, after all.

Dimitri flashes Alek a sinister grin. "I'm glad you asked." He says, hopping up on the stage. "Gentlemen," He booms, extending his arms out in a grand gesture. "It's a new era for our business. Trafficking guns and drugs to make ends meet is a thing of the past. The profits don't always outweigh the costs and frankly, why should we continue slumming it with local street gangs when there are other more profitable ventures to explore. Sex is the future. The profits are exponential and the opportunity cost is minimal if you manage your resources properly. It's no secret that Los Angeles is The West Coast's most profitable territory to date, and that is all thanks to the underground sex clubs I established years ago. I've spoken with the council and they agree that it's time the rest of the west coast syndicates follow suit."

The silence that falls over the room is deafening. It's an unspoken rule within The Organization that we keep our money out of women and children. Sex work is one thing, but we all know what Dimitri's really talking about is sex slavery. It's easy to keep your "opportunity cost" so minimal when your entire staff is working for zero pay.

Andrei, the muscle of The Forsaken, jumps up from his seat and slams his palm against the table. "Did Oleg even sign off on this shit?" He asks, furrowing his brows. "Who the hell do you think you are coming in here and telling us what to do with our cities?"

Dimitri lets out a vile, sadistic laugh as he slowly shakes his head. "You're right. Oleg wouldn't have signed off on this, but his opinion no longer matters. He's dead." He says, leveling his eyes on Andrei as his smile fades. "And I'm afraid, old friend, so are you."

Before anyone can do anything to stop him, Dimitri whips out his gun and pulls the trigger. The bullet zips across the room and rips into the center of Andrei's forehead with deadly precision. Blood drips down his face as the man's heavy body crumples to the ground and the rest of the room erupts in chaos.

Every other man in the room draws his gun and begins shouting as the distrust in the air boils over. The three of us sit and watch as Dimitri's eyes glimmer with excitement. We're used to him and his calculated cruelty, but it's obvious that for most of the men in the room, this is their first real taste of who Dimitri really is, beyond his careful veneer.

"I'm the new head of West Coast operations." Dimitri calls out over the melody of protests and accusations. "If any of you have a problem with that, now is the time to speak up."

The sounds in the room die down as soon as they come to terms with what this all means.

"Questions?" Dimitri asks, flashing the room a broad grin. "No? I didn't think so. Now if you'll excuse me." He says, tucking his gun back into its holster before jumping off of the stage to pick up his coat. "I've got some personal business to take care of. I expect full status reports on your new business ventures in no longer than three months. Have a good night, gentlemen."

With that parting statement, Dimitri exits the building nearly as quickly as he arrived. Leaving the mess he made behind for us to clean.

Pushing drugs and running our various legitimate businesses has been working for us for the last 7 years and The Organization never once complained about the 40% overhead they took in.

This change is personal and is Dimitri's way of separating himself from his predecessor. But enforcing a change like this is overkill and will garner him more enemies than he can handle. Everyone in this room can see that the man who was just standing before us is nothing like Oleg and, no matter how hard he tries, he never will be.

I release an exasperated breath and rub my temples just to make sure my brain is hearing him correctly. "What did you just s… say?" I ask, peering closer to his face.

Ezra stares at his zippo, flicking the lid open and closed, over and over again. His mouth is pressed in a hard line and his eyes look dead inside.

"She's gone." He repeats, refusing to look up at the three of us. The second we opened the front door, we found him like this at the foot of the stairs. Atlas tried to get him to talk, but for the first couple of minutes, he refused to say anything. Just sat there playing with his lighter. It wasn't until Cyrus screamed at him that we finally got him to say those words.

"What the fuck do you mean she's gone?" Atlas hisses, glaring at him. "You were supposed to watch her. What happened?"

"Mitri happened." Cyrus spits, pacing the floor. "I knew that meeting was just a fucking distraction. The asshole did something to make her leave."

"It wasn't Dimitri." Ezra says, finally glaring up at the three of us as he clenches his jaw. "It was me."

"It was you?" I ask, glaring at him. "What does that even f… fucking mean?"

"She wanted to see the monster." He says dismissively. "So I let her."

"Did you hurt her?" Atlas asks, flaring his nostrils as an eerie calm overtakes his entire demeanor.

Ezra solemnly shakes his head. "Not in the way you think."

"We need to go find her." Cyrus says as he continues to pace. "It isn't safe for her out there."

"She made her choice." Ezra says, standing up as he tucks

his zippo away. "She doesn't want us and it's time we fucking accepted it. She was only ever supposed to be a toy. Just consider her permanently broken."

I look at Atlas and Cy, and they both look conflicted. Like they actually buy into Ezra's bullshit. *This is stupid.* He can't do this. He can't just make a decision about our lives like this.

"F... fuck that." I snarl, grabbing my keys. "I'm going out t... to find her whether you like it or not. I'm n... not done with her. N... Not by a long shot."

"Tristan," Ezra calls out and the ice in his voice stops me in my tracks, "if you bring her back to this house, I will kill her. Her blood will be on your hands and if you think I give a fuck about the repercussions, you're wrong. I don't fear death, I welcome it."

The fire within me slowly extinguishes, as my shoulders slump. I may want Stevie back, but there's no way in hell I'm putting her in danger. As much as I hate to admit it, Ezra's right. If I bring her back here and he hurts her, I'll never be able to live with myself. Right now, the safest place for her is as far away from us as possible.

TWENTY-TWO

Stevie

Two Days Later

I STUDY him as he cuts two juicy slices off a lemon and carefully sets them on the edges of our ice-filled glasses. He wraps his fingers around the ice-cold bottle of Pellegrino and just as he begins twisting the cap off, a surprise hiss of gas escapes the bottle. He jumps back a little before a hint of a smile touches his lips. He feels silly for his reaction and as a soft blush stains his cheeks, he slowly shakes his head.

It's a minuscule sign of his humanity, but that doesn't stop me from envying him for it. I hate how numb I've become. How I never let anything hurt me. I hate that the second I feel pain coming, my gut instinct is to run. And as much as I try to deny it, isn't that what I'm doing right now? Running?

He finishes splashing the bubbly concoction into our glasses and gently places the bottle on the mosaic tiled table perched between our lounge chairs. He takes a step back and offers us a gentle bow, almost as if to say "All yours."

"That'll be all, Charles." Melanie says, stabbing a stainless steel straw into her glass before wrapping her ruby red lips around it. "Thank you."

I offer Charles a sham of a smile to thank him, but it's the only thing I can muster. It pales in comparison to the genuine smile on his face, but he accepts it anyway and retreats back into the house.

"You know, most people would kill to lounge by a pool like this and here you are, looking like someone killed your goddamn puppy."

I let out a half-hearted laugh. "Is it that obvious?" I'm normally good at hiding my emotions. At shielding myself from the rest of the world. But even after 48 hours to fester, this cut hurts more than anything I've ever felt before. More than losing Alex.

"Isn't this what you wanted?" She prods. "To get away from them for good."

"It was." I stammer. "I mean it is. I just… You're probably the last person I should tell all this to. Your father is the leader of their rival for god's sake."

Melanie takes another slow sip of her sparkling water before responding. "I'm not my father, Stevie." She says, taking on a more serious tone. "And despite what you may think, The Reapers have always been good friends of mine. I care about them, and strangely enough, I care about you, too. You can talk to me. And I mean, it's not like you have anyone else to talk to."

"You're right." I say, exhaling a deep breath. "Okay, honestly? It still doesn't make sense to me. Why would Ezra kill my sister?"

Melanie pulls off sunglasses and glares at me. "Babe, he's Ezra. He's been through a lot of shit. Does he ever have a reason for acting the way he does?"

"I don't know." I say, gnawing on my lower lip. "Something still doesn't sit right with me about the whole Ezra thing. After Alex disappeared, he was out nearly every night. If his end goal was to get closer to me, why the hell would he distance himself so much? Why not cozy up to me while I'm freaking out about Alex? I mean, for all he knew, I'd never find out who took her. So why not take advantage of the alone time?"

"That's a good point." She says, sipping on her Pellegrino. "But you found his jacket. If that's not him being caught red-handed, I don't know what is."

"Yeah."

"And you said it yourself, he confessed."

Did he?

"I mean, he said her blood was on his hands."

"And that doesn't strike you as a confession?"

"Not really."

Melanie sets her glass down, leans back into her lounge chair, and closes her eyes to soak in the sun's powerful rays.

"You know what I think?" She murmurs. "I think you're looking for a reason to forgive him. You want Ezra to have a conscience, to think and behave like a normal person would. But babe, he's not normal. There's nothing underneath the beautiful shell but a cold black heart."

Mel's phone dings and I'm literally saved by the bell. Maybe she's right. Maybe I'm searching for the good in Ezra that just isn't there.

Out of nowhere, Melanie drops her phone, and the sound of it crashing against the ground jolts me from my thoughts.

I stare at Melanie, but she doesn't make a move to pick it up. She just sits there, staring off into the distance.

"Is everything okay?" I ask, studying her sullen face. "You look like you're going to be sick."

"I'm fine." She clips, slipping on her sunglasses as her lips form a tight line. "My fingers were still slippery from the pool. No big deal. Should we head back inside and grab some food?"

The way she's acting is strange, but I just place the blame on too much time in the sun and follow her back into the house.

"I wasn't expecting this, you know..." She says, taking a seat on one of her kitchen barstools.

"Expecting what?" I ask, cocking a brow as I take a seat on the opposite side.

"To like you." She confesses, keeping her eyes on the marble countertop. "I thought you were a bitch and when you asked to come here, my gut instinct was to tell you to fuck off.

But in the last couple of days, I've realized we have a lot in common."

"What changed your mind?"

Melanie hesitates. "I got a text. One that I should've dug deeper into, but I was mad at you and I didn't give a fuck about what he had planned for you. But now I do."

"What are you talking about?" I ask, cocking my head at her.

"Dimitri's coming for you. He's planning on taking you home. I think it's his way of forcing the guys to owe him a favor."

Her phone dings and my heart jumps into my throat.

"That's him." Mel says, standing up from her chair. "I'm sorry, Stevie."

I jump up from my seat and stop her. "Just don't let him in," I stammer, "or tell him I'm not here."

Melanie lingers at the counter and gives me a sad smile. "I know you don't fully understand this yet," she says, buzzing him in through the gate on her phone, "but no one says no to Dimitri Evanoff."

Time stands still as I watch in disbelief as Melanie slides the front door open and Dimitri steps through the door. His powerful body stunts Mels in comparison and I mindlessly wonder if that's how insignificant I look when I'm next to The Reapers.

This man has gone from enemy to ally to whatever-the-hell-he-thinks-this-is, so swiftly it's hard to know what to feel about him. But regardless of our complicated past, if he's here to take me home against my will, he isn't a fucking friend and neither is Mel.

"You've had your fun." Dimitri says, looking down at me. "But it's time to go home, Kroshka."

"No." I say, shaking my head in disbelief. "I'm not ready to face them yet. It's only been a couple of days, I need more time."

"Sweet naïve, Kroshka," he chastises, shaking his head as his large hand grabs a hold of my jaw and squishes my lips, "that isn't your home anymore. Your home is with me."

I stare at him, horrified as shock overtakes my body. *What the fuck is he talking about?* I try to jerk out of his hold, but when I do, he squeezes me even tighter. Painfully so. I start kicking and punching and flailing against him, but it's pointless. I'm helpless to fight him off.

"Wait." Melanie calls out, seeing the exchange going on between us. "That wasn't part of the plan."

Dimitri slides his hand around my throat, turns his head, and glares at her. "That was always part of my plan."

Melanie's eyes flash from him to me and then back to him. "No." She says, shaking her head indignantly. "I'm not letting you take her."

Dimitri laughs, and as he does, he crushes my throat and lifts me up in an expression of his power. "She belongs to me now." He hisses, staring at me as my vision blurs. "And I'm afraid you don't have a say in any of this."

"Charles!" Melanie screams and the next five seconds happen so fast I can barely keep up.

Charles charges into the room with his gun drawn and ready for war. The look on his face is cold, dark, and lethal and he levels his gun at Dimitri with deadly precision. Charles is fast, but Dimitri is faster. Before Charles can pull the trigger, Dimitri uses his free hand to whip his own gun out and fires a bullet straight into the center of Charles' stomach.

Melanie releases a heart-wrenching scream as she watches his body slowly crumple to the ground. She levels her teary eyes at Dimitri and with no warning; she leaps for him.

Melanie crashes into Dimitri and all of her rage and pain explodes out of her as she forces a powerful kick straight into his balls. Dimitri curses on impact and drops me to the floor as Melanie continues to punch and kick and slap and claw at him. I gasp for air as I try to scramble to my feet and try to help Melanie. *This man is a fucking lunatic and he'll kill her if I don't stop him.*

The two of them are tussling now, struggling over control of Dimitri's gun. I race for Charles' gun, but I only make it two steps when I hear a loud bang go off. I snap my head around in time to lock eyes with Melanie as she collapses to the floor. As blood blooms across her chest, she looks at me with so much sadness in her eyes it hurts. *Fuck. Fuck. Fuck.*

"Run." She croaks, glancing towards the front door.

And I do. I bolt for Melanie's front door and I don't look back. They need help, and the only way any of us are getting out of here alive is if I escape. As my heart thunders in my chest, my bare feet pound against the cold tile, and I race for the exit. I can't focus on anything else around me. All I see is the door and I'm so close, I'm afraid that if I blink my eyes, it'll disappear and I'll realize it was all just a figment of my imagination. But I make it, and it is real. I reach for the handle, and the second I feel the cool metal graze my fingertips, something hard smashes against my head and everything goes dark.

WRATH OF THE REAPERS EXCERPT

Stevie

THE AIR IS DIFFERENT IN THIS PLACE. STAGNANT AND THICK. Laced with this underlying scent of decay that only years of neglect could bring. It's hot and impossibly humid too. I woke up a few hours ago with a parched mouth and nearly every inch of my body coated in a thin layer of sweat.

It's dark. So purely pitch black that it's almost impossible to see anything in front of me. It's the kind of darkness nightmares are made of. The kind of darkness you can't stare at for too long, not without panic setting it.

What is this place?

From what I can tell, I'm not injured, and aside from the tight ropes biting into my ankles and wrists and the pounding headache that still hasn't gone away, I feel little pain.

I have to give it to them. Whoever tied me to this chair knew what they were doing. I've been testing the binds since I woke up and all I've managed to do is rub my skin raw.

I'm not sure how long I sat here drifting in and out of sleep before I came to. Minutes? Hours? Days? My memory is hazy and the longer I sit here, the harder it is to keep track. I don't know what Dimitri wants from me or why the hell he's left me here. *All I really know is I need to get the hell out of here.*

THE NEXT TIME I wake up I try to search the darkness again, but there's still nothing discernible about this place. Just four dark walls cast in even darker shadows.

Staring out into the void feels like I'm drowning. Like I'm sinking beneath the depths of thick, murky water and no matter how hard I try to claw up to the surface, I can't. There's no light to guide me. Just darkness. All-consuming, inescapable darkness.

I should be used to this feeling. I think bitterly as I give up on the search and close my eyes once more.

I've been drowning for a while now. In guilt. In fear. In emotions I was never really equipped to handle. And being in this place only seems to amplify that feeling. Almost as if the dark solitude is forcing me to face everything I've been trying to avoid.

I'm not a good person. I used to think I was, but after everything I've done, how can I possibly still believe that?

My little sister is dead because of me. Ezra may have been the one to pull the trigger, but Alex would've never been on his radar if I didn't selfishly put her there.

Same with Melanie and Charles. They were the closest thing I had to friends, and they died trying to save me from a lunatic I stupidly lured in. The Reapers warned me about Dimitri and I always knew there was something off with him. I was just too selfish and bullheaded to see how dangerous he was until it was too late.

I've hurt the people closest to me and if my dad were alive, he would be so fucking disappointed in the person I've become. Cold. Ruthless. Deceitful. That's not the kind of woman he raised me to be. Then again, maybe that's the biggest problem in all of this.

I've spent my whole life trying to be good and live up to the standards my father set for me. But maybe I've just been fighting a losing battle all along. Maybe hurting others is in my DNA. *After all, I'm not just his daughter, I'm hers too.*

A FEW DAYS *later*

. . .

I'M DRIFTING. Floating somewhere between being asleep and awake when I hear the distinct sound of the lock on my door shift. It's a tiny disruption. One I probably shouldn't notice. But I've always been a light sleeper and being in this place has trained me to stay vigilant.

I keep my eyes shut as the overhead lights flicker on and the door slowly creeps open. Pretending to sleep never stops them, but I'm greedy for any moments of reprieve I can get.

"Good morning." A chilling voice calls out, cutting into the silence that normally fills the room. Even without looking, I know who it is. Dimitri's right hand man, or as I like to refer to him as, The Zombie.

I'm sure he has a real name, one Dimitri's called out on more than one occasion, but I refuse to learn it. Fuck humanizing the enemy. Besides, learning anything else about him feels a little morbid considering I plan on slaughtering him.

The Zombie's footfalls are slow and methodical as he approaches me, almost as if he's purposely taking his time to scare me, but I stuff the fear down before it can take root. *He's not worth it.*

"I know you aren't sleeping." He taunts, stepping deeper into the basement. "If I'm honest, I couldn't sleep either. I stayed up all night thinking about you."

His little confession makes me want to gag. Having him visit me is bad enough, but just the idea of this sick fuck thinking about me on his downtime makes me want to scrub my skin off.

He stops moving, and for a moment; the silence is deafening. I try to listen for him, but the only sound coming through is the rhythmic pounding of my own heartbeat.

"Open your fucking eyes." He snaps, reappearing within inches of me.

Before I can even think about following his orders, he latches onto the back of my head and pulls. Yanking my hair back so violently that it feels like my scalp is literally being ripped off.

I don't scream, because fuck giving him the satisfaction, but the sudden burst of pain is blinding. I have no choice but to move to relieve some of the pressure.

I try to inch closer to his hand, but the ropes around my wrists keep me practically glued to the chair and I have no choice but to sit and wait until he's done for the pain to stop.

I've lost count of how many times he's greeted me like this in the last few days. Three times? Five times? Nine? It's hard to discern one memory from another in this place.

"You have no one to blame but yourself for that." He says as he finally loosens his hold and relieves some of the pressure. "Now how about you be a good girl and do as I ask?"

Begrudgingly, I force my eyes open and glare at the monster standing above me. *Jesus.* I don't think I'll ever get used to seeing him this up close. I nicknamed him The Zombie for a reason. The man looks like Dimitri ripped him out of a fucking horror movie, and not the psychological thriller kind, the gory, gives-you-nightmares kind.

His shiny bald head gleams under the fluorescent light and his sickly pale skin is so thin it's almost transparent. He has over-exaggerated features that only add to the air of other-worldliness about him, with cold, lifeless eyes, a prominent nose, an oversized mouth, and jagged, silver scars covering nearly every inch of his skin. He cocks his head as he takes stock of me, a cold chill instantly climbs up my spine. *I hate the effect he has on me.*

"I said good morning." He hisses, gritting his teeth as he glares down at me. "It isn't very polite of you not to say anything back."

I almost scoff at his words. He wants *me* to be polite? He can't be serious.

I blink at him, like he's the stupidest person I've ever met, because, well he just might be and his lip curls in response.

Wow… he isn't kidding.

I guess it makes sense considering how deranged his boss is.

Dimitri swears his intentions are pure. That he orchestrated all of this, not to punish me, but to help me see how *generous* his offer is. He's convinced I'll come to thank him for this in the end. Now, if that doesn't speak to how delusional the man truly is, I don't know what will.

"What's the matter?" The Zombie asks, grabbing ahold of my face and letting his hot breath dance across my skin. "Cat got your tongue?"

He painfully squishes my cheeks together, using his filthy fingernails to dig deeper and deeper into the skin until I have no choice but to pry my mouth open and relieve the pressure.

"Nope." He says, staring at my tongue with a smirk. "Still there."

He runs his thumb across my bottom lip and I dig my nails into the arms of my wooden chair to stop myself from repelling. "It would be a shame if your bad attitude forced me to cut out that pretty little tongue of yours."

He's bluffing. Dimitri lets him get away with a lot, but

he'd never let him cause me any permanent damage. Not because he cares about me, but because if I agree to his offer, I'll need to look like I'm doing so willingly. Cuts and bruises can heal in a few days, but anything more severe will raise some serious red flags.

I can't smell much of anything, thanks to the mixture of blood and sweat permeating in the air, but I make a show of dry-heaving from the stench of his breath just to fuck with him. It's juvenile, but part of surviving means doing whatever I can to get under his skin. After all, every second I'm in his head is a second he isn't beating into mine.

"You think you're funny?" He snaps, practically snarling the word at me, as if doing so will somehow scare me into answering him.

I can't help but laugh as I lick at my cracked lips. *Actually, yeah.* I think I'm pretty hilarious. All things considered.

He cocks his head at me, like he's actually expecting an explanation, and my laughter only grows. *What part of I'm not fucking cooperating are you not getting?*

I feel the sting of my lips splitting, but I can't stop. It's just so fucking ridiculous. *Look at me.* I'm bruised and beaten. Covered in a mixture of dried blood and my own filth because I'm refusing to comply with their demands. What the hell makes him think that this interaction is going to be any different?

Without warning, his fist strikes out, smashing into the side of my face with enough force to break skin. My head painfully jerks to the side and a familiar burn ignites across my cheek as the fresh taste of copper fills my mouth.

Fuck.

He continues his assault on me, like a rabid fucking animal, and I wish I could say I'm surprised at how hard he's hitting me, but I'm not. After spending so much time in this place, I've learned there's nothing Dimitri's men love more than making me bleed.

I know I should stop this. I should just give in and avoid all of this pain. But I can't let Dimitri win. *I won't.*

After a while, his blows lull to a stop and he backs away to assess the damage. "My, my, my…" He says, smiling down at me. "That looks like it hurts."

I can't see the damage he inflicted but I can feel it. The left side of my face is throbbing and I can already feel my eye swelling shut, but it's my head that I'm really worried about.

The torture sessions with him are always bad, but they never leaving me feeling like this. I must've really pissed him off this time and if I don't do something to stop him, he's going to kill me. Intentionally or not.

I release a whimper and force myself to start crying, doing what I can to attract his attention. It's calculated, but it's the first sign of defeat any of them have seen since the torture sessions started. Instead of being suspicious, like he should be, he looks at me and his face is practically beaming with delight.

"Are you finally ready to agree?" He asks, cutting right to the chase. "We're just getting started, but it doesn't look like you can handle much more."

I give him a small nod and keep my head low, playing up my defeat to the fullest.

He immediately jumps into action. He whips his phone out and when I see him dial a number and press the phone to his ear, a hint of a smile plays on my lips. *Good boy.*

He mumbles out a few Russian words I don't understand as he paces back and forth. And just as quickly as he started the call, he ends it.

For a while it's just the two of us, and even though my head is down, I can still feel his eyes on me. Studying me, like he's still not quite sure if he believes me. It's too late for him to change his mind. The call's already been made.

A few moments later, the door slides open and another person enters the room. They don't say anything as they take their position behind me, but their notable silence tells me everything I need to know. *It's Dimitri.*

Dimitri and his men have been trying to break me for days. Rotating shifts every few hours to torture me, feed me, and escort me to bathroom in that order. Ironically enough, Dimitri only shows up to feed me, so the fact that he's here now means my shitty acting actually worked.

"Speak." The Zombie says, his voice laced with pride. "We don't have all day."

I slowly nod my head and gesture for The Zombie to come closer. Like the coward he is; he looks to Dimitri for permission before making a move. It's hard not to laugh at the irony. He wants permission to approach me, but beating the shit out of me without so much as a warning is a-okay.

Dimitri gives him a firm nod and, like the perfect little lap dog he is, The Zombie eagerly approaches. As I watch him move towards me, I can almost see his thoughts written all over his face. He thinks he's won. That all of his violence has finally forced me to comply, and damn, does it make me giddy just thinking about how wrong he is. *Enjoy this moment of bliss, you stupid fuck.*

As soon as he's perched beside me, I make a move to

speak. I can even feel the phantom words dance on the tip of my tongue, but instead of uttering the words of agreement both of them are desperately wanting to hear, I gather all the blood in my mouth and spray it, splattering bloody saliva all over the side of his face.

I watch with wild amusement as he implodes. His entire body vibrates with the need to hurt me and it's obvious he's seconds away from losing it.

I laugh, because I can't help it, and the sound of my laughter only seems to fuel his rage. His head snaps up and the look on his face is the most sub-human thing I've ever seen. He wants to kill me, I can see it in his eyes and fuck, it feels good to know I'm the one who's pushed him there.

Looks like I broke you first, asshole.

Within seconds, Dimitri is between us, acting as a human shield as he shoves his rabid henchman away. To anyone else, his actions would look heroic, like a small part of him cares and wants to protect me. But that's just another one of his illusions. I've spent too much time in this place to mistake his interference as anything other than an act of self-preservation.

"I'm sorry to waste your time, boss." The Zombie huffs, speaking to Dimitri as he continues to glare daggers at me. "I thought I had her."

Dimitri shakes his head slowly before palming the man's blood-splattered face in his hands. "You did good, Ivan." He assures, releasing his hold as he leads him towards the exit. "This one just needs a little more convincing than most. But she'll break. Eventually, they all do."

I narrow my eyes at him, but say nothing as I watch his henchman quietly exit the room.

The door closes, and part of me knows I should feel better.

The Zombie was on the verge of killing me, and I should be relieved that he's gone. But when I look at Dimitri and see the strange gleam in his icy blue eyes, I know the real torture is only beginning. I'm not sure what he's planning, but one thing's for sure... *this is going to be a long fucking night...*

STAY IN TOUCH

To stay to up to date with my latest releases, announcements, and book recommendations, don't forget to subscribe to my newsletter at www.jessahalliwell.com

BOOKS BY JESSA

Fear The Reapers
Book One of The Reapers of Caspian Hills

Queen of The Reapers
Book Two of The Reapers of Caspian Hills

Wrath of The Reapers
Book Three of The Reapers of Caspian Hills

Brutal Enemies
A Dark Mafia Reverse Harem Romance
Release Date: TBD

Chronicles of The Damned
A Vampire Romance Charity Anthology
Releasing October 1, 2022

A NOTE FROM JESSA

Queen of The Reapers was all about showing Stevie's rise and subsequent fall from grace.

In this book, she was frustrating and a lot of the times, you were probably questioning if you still wanted to root for her.

But in order to make her feel as real as possible, I had to get into her head and really think about what she would do and how she would react to the situations she's thrown into.

Stevie's human. And humans are frustrating. We fuck up. We make stupid decisions in the heat of the moment and we deal with the consequences of our actions. We don't always mean what we say and we don't always say what we mean. We're flawed. Perfectly, stupidly, flawed.

I know this cliffy stings, but I promise book three will be worth the wait. I can't wait for you all to find out how their story concludes.

xoxo,
    Jessa

ABOUT JESSA

Jessa Halliwell is a Reverse Harem Romance Author who writes about angsty, torturous love mixed with a dash of danger. She loves writing romance only slightly more than she loves reading it. She's been known to binge read novels then spend the rest of the day sulking over the massive book hangover.

Jessa resides in Northern California with her boyfriend and her feisty Chihuahua named Juice. When she isn't writing, you can find her obsessing over her skincare routine, drinking an unhealthy amount of hibiscus tea, or probably crying over a really good book.

Follow me on tiktok: @jessahalliwellauthor

Join my Facebook Readers Groups: **Halliwell's Harem** and **Dark & Dangerous Reverse Harem Readers**

Printed in Great Britain
by Amazon